ALL YOUR TOMORROWS

J. NATHAN

Edited by Stephanie Elliot
Cover Design by Y'all. That Graphic.

First Edition May 2023

For my son.
May all your tomorrows be filled
with love, laughter, and luck.

CHAPTER 1
December

"Lucy!" I called out the name on the cup of hot chocolate and set it down on the counter.

A little girl bounced over to the counter to grab it with her mittened hands. "Thanks," she said before returning to her mom who waited near the Christmas tree by the front door. The bell chimed as they walked outside, leaving the café empty once again.

"What are you up to this weekend?" Daci asked.

I spun around to face my boss standing at the cappuccino machine on the back counter, her red apron complementing her wavy black hair. "I already cleaned that," I assured her.

"Of course you did," she said with a knowing grin. Daci had owned the café for the past five years—since she graduated from Lancaster University. Her dad had promised her he'd help her open a business if she made straight As throughout college. Though, he probably never expected her to open a café, nor would he have approved of what took place through the sparkly strands of curtains separating the café from the room in the back. "You didn't answer my question," she persisted. "I asked what you're doing this weekend."

"Just staying in," I said.

"Girl. You're hot and single. College is supposed to be the best time of your life."

I rolled my eyes. She knew about the betrayal I'd gone through over the summer. So, I knew she was just trying to get me back out there. But once you'd been deceived by two people you trusted implicitly, your walls just went up and were difficult to break back down.

"I'm gonna take out the trash," she said before disappearing into the back room.

Motion by the front door snagged my attention. We were nearing nine—closing time—and I really wanted to go home. I turned to see who had come in and my head hitched back. A guy around my age moved toward the counter in low hung jeans and a black hoodie. If I were moving, my steps would've faltered. He was *that* good looking. "Can I help you?" I asked, trying to play it cool as he stepped up to the counter.

He glanced around, his green eyes moving to the curtains in the rear of the café before cutting back to mine. "I'm looking for someone," he said, his voice raspy and unlike the southern drawls I was used to hearing in Virginia.

Of course he was meeting someone. He was way too hot not to be. "Oh, okay," I said. "Would you like to order now or wait until they arrive?"

His eyes narrowed, seemingly confused by my question.

"We're closing in ten minutes," I explained. "So you might want to place your order now."

"I'm not meeting someone," he explained. "I'm looking for Nora."

My head retracted as unexpected warmth flooded my insides. "I'm Nora."

Relief washed over his features. "You are?"

I nodded, waiting for the punchline.

"Can we sit down?" he asked.

I glanced around, totally confused. Had Daci set me up? Was she watching on the cameras in the back and feeling proud of herself right now? She was always prying into my private life. Had she finally had it with my non-existent dating life?

Here goes nothing.

"Sure," I said, moving around the counter. Once I stood in front of him, I realized he was a good six inches taller than me and I needed to tip my head up to meet his green-eyed gaze. He moved toward a table by the window, and as I followed, I tugged my hair band out of my low ponytail and subtly shook out my dark waves. He slipped into a seat and I sat down across from him.

"I'm not really sure where to begin," he said, his hands folding in front of him on the table.

"How about with your name," I smiled. "You know mine."

"Kyler."

I smiled. "Nice name."

He nodded, though his eyes seemed to be avoiding mine.

"Did Daci ask you to come here?" I blurted out.

"Who's Daci?"

"Nora, I'm heading out." Daci stepped out from the back room. I expected her to apologize for interrupting—like she hadn't set me up. But she didn't. "You taking a break?" she asked showing no indication that she recognized Kyler.

"Just for a minute," I said, trying to read the room.

"You better come in on Monday with some stories about your weekend. Stories involving *hot* guys," she said.

I laughed nervously. I couldn't believe she'd say something like that when a totally hot guy was seated right across from me.

She grabbed her keys from the cash register and moved to the door. The bell chimed as she pulled open the door. "See you Monday." And then she was gone.

That's when a cold chill rushed up the back of my neck, and my shoulders fell lax. My eyes shot back to Kyler. "How long have you been dead?"

CHAPTER 2

"Excuse me?" Kyler asked.

"Why didn't I know? I should've known. When you came in, the bell on the door didn't ring. There were no footsteps. And then Daci didn't see you." I dropped my forehead into my palm. I'd been so distracted by his good looks, I'd been completely off my game.

"Are you okay?" Kyler asked.

I sighed as I let my hand fall. "Sorry. This isn't supposed to be about me. What can I do for you?"

"I have no idea."

I tipped my head to the side, taking in his lips which were slightly turned up in the corners even though he wasn't smiling. "But you came to me."

"I heard you could help," he said.

"I have to know what I'm helping with," I explained.

He looked down at himself, his dark hair falling over his forehead as he did. "Why am I like this?"

"Like what?"

"Here…but not here," he explained.

I lowered my voice, trying to tread gently. They didn't all understand how it worked—hell I didn't always understand how it worked. "Because you died," I explained. "Do you know how it happened?"

He shook his head.

My lips twisted regrettably. It always sucked when they didn't remember. I considered my next question carefully, realizing if he didn't know how he died, he likely wasn't keen on the idea that he was indeed dead.

"I find myself walking around town. Visiting places I used to visit. But no one can see me. Not one person. Until you."

"I'm a medium."

"Yeah, I overheard someone saying you see ghosts."

"Spirits," I corrected him. "And only when I allow it. That's why you surprised me. I didn't open my mind to it—at least I thought I didn't." I shrugged. "Anyway, spirits come to me in all different ways. Some I hear. Some show me visions in my head. But you. You're clear as day. The weird thing is you don't have that almost-glow that lets me know you're not actually real."

"I feel real," he said. "Until I speak and no one responds."

"I'm sorry. That's got to be awful. How long has it been going on?"

His eyes drifted up as if he needed to think about his answer. "Too long."

I pulled my phone from my apron pocket and called up a search. "What's your last name?"

"Fletcher."

I searched his name on my phone. "This article says you were in a car accident." I glanced up, looking for any sign of recollection. His eyes narrowed, but he seemed to be unable to recall. "Why can't I remember?"

"Maybe you blocked it out," I offered before glancing back down at the article and reading a little more. "You were in the car with your girlfriend."

"I had a girlfriend?"

"I guess so. Her name is Melanie."

He shook his head, unable to recall the information I was telling him. "Why can't I remember that?"

I shrugged. "It says she walked away with minor injuries, but you—"

"I what?"

"You were in a coma."

"A coma?" he asked.

I stopped reading and looked him in the eyes. I could see pain there. I could see the frustration that came with not remembering.

"Why haven't I gone…" he glanced up.

"Some spirits linger. Some appear when they choose to."

"Why linger?"

"Unfinished business usually."

I glanced back down at the article. "It says your accident was over Christmas break last year."

"I always came home for the holiday. Did it say I was driving?"

I nodded, uncomfortable at having to share that information.

"Did we hit another car? Were other people hurt?"

I continued reading more of the article. "You drove off the road—off a bridge," I corrected.

"What?"

"It said the road must've been slippery. You were stuck underwater in the car, but you helped your girlfriend get free."

"Jesus Christ," he murmured.

"You saved her," I said, meeting his eyes and hoping to relieve some of the guilt I was seeing there. "You should feel happy about that." I looked back to the article, but the alarm on my phone went off, beeping loudly and signifying closing time. I jumped up and moved to the front door, peering out onto the street. A few cars were parked on either side. But the bookstore, candy shop, and boutique had all closed at eight, so no one walked around the normally busy shopping street.

"Do you want me to leave?" Kyler asked.

I glanced over my shoulder as I locked the front door. "No. I just don't plan on making coffee for any drunk college kids." I flipped off the main lights, but the soft glow from the under-the-counter lights and the Christmas tree in the front window kept the shop dimly lit. "Some of them make their way over here."

"Aren't you in college?" he asked.

"I'm a senior at Lancaster. I finished my exams early so I'm already on break. Most are still here until Wednesday." I moved back to the table and sat down. "Did you go to Lancaster U?"

He shook his head. "Florida."

A long silence passed. I'd just dropped a lot on him so I wasn't about to usher him out or press him for more information he didn't seem to remember.

"I can't visit my family," he finally said. "I've tried to get close to our house, but I just can't seem to get there."

"Sometimes spirits get stuck and can only travel to certain places. I'm not sure why that is."

He looked down, and I couldn't imagine not being able to see my mom—to get to the one place I needed to get to.

"I can go over to your house tomorrow. Maybe you'll be able to see your family through me."

His eyes shot up. "You'd do that?"

"If you'd like me to," I said.

"Will it work?"

"I guess we'll find out tomorrow," I said.

"I really appreciate this, Nora." The sound of him saying my name seemed so natural, rolling off his tongue so effortlessly. "I'm sorry I've taken up so much of your time. Can I walk you out?" he offered.

Sadly, it was the best offer I'd had in a long time. "Sure." I pushed back my chair and stood. His chair didn't push back as he stood. It was strange that spirits could move through some objects like doors and walls, but could sit on chairs or other solid furniture without passing through them.

I walked to the counter and shut down the register. I grabbed my backpack from under the counter and walked toward the back.

Kyler followed me through the strands of sparkly curtains to my space in the back of the café. Daci had given me the room to meet with "clients." Though I had the "ability" to see and talk to spirits since I was nine, I'd only been doing readings for a year. Most customers who came into the café had no idea what I did when I wasn't working as a barista. My appointments were scheduled online.

"Other spirits have been in here, haven't they?" Kyler asked as he took in the wooden table and the plaid cushioned chairs where I connected people with their deceased loved ones.

"Yeah."

"Is it weird?"

"What?"

"Seeing spirits?"

"I've gotten used to it. Most of them are respectful and don't bother me when I don't want to be bothered."

"Did I bother you?" he asked.

I laughed. "No. You were very polite."

He smirked, and I realized it had been a while since a guy looked at me that way.

I took him through the back room, past cardboard boxes filled with coffee cups, plastic covers, straws, and stirrers. I removed my apron and hung it on the coat rack, then grabbed my coat and pulled it on. I wrapped my plaid scarf around my neck and threw my backpack over my shoulders. I opened the door and Kyler stepped outside. Once he did, I turned around and locked the door behind us, punching in the alarm code to set it before leaving.

"So, where's your car?" he asked, taking in the empty parking lot.

"I walk to work. My house is just a few blocks away."

"Lead the way," he said.

I smiled as I pulled my gloves out of my pocket and slipped them on. "It's getting cold."

"I can't feel it. Like, I know it should be cold, but I feel nothing."

Unsure what to say, I began walking through the alleyway between the café and the gift shop next door and stepped out onto the sidewalk.

Kyler buried his hands in his hoodie pocket as he walked alongside me. We slowly made our way down the empty sidewalk, passing each window that was aglow with tiny strands of white lights for the upcoming holiday. "Do you like being a medium?"

"I don't really have a choice."

"Doesn't mean you have to like it," he said.

"I like helping people," I said.

"What are you majoring in at school?" he asked.

"Child psychology."

"Of course you are," he teased.

"That obvious, huh?"

"That obvious," he agreed.

"What were you studying?" I asked.

"Sports medicine."

"Of course you were," I teased.

"That obvious?" he asked.

I laughed. "That obvious."

I turned onto my street which was known as one of the party streets in our college town. Most houses were lit up and we could hear music blaring as we walked by.

"You live in one of these?" Kyler asked, eyeing the massive two-story houses that had seen better days. Some boasted frat letters over the front doors, while others had old beat-up sofas on the lawns.

I shook my head. Izzy and I lived in a small cape at the end of the block that didn't quite fit in with the party houses on the main strip. It had been intentional. We didn't want to be stuck in the middle of the party zone—especially since I'd be alone most of the time with Izzy traveling so much. "See that white picket fence?" I pointed in front of us.

He squinted. "No."

I laughed. "At the very end."

Given it was dark at the end of the street—and he didn't say anything, I assumed he couldn't see it.

"My best friend Izzy and I live there," I explained.

"Who are you talking to?"

I turned in the direction of the girl who'd spoken.

She was a short blonde with a red cup in her hand staring at me from the lawn of a frat house where a loud party raged inside. "Are you wasted?" she asked, her bare feet stumbling around.

"No, but you clearly are," Kyler said.

I stifled a grin, knowing she couldn't hear him. "Yeah. Totally wasted," I lied. "Killer party, huh?"

"Killer," she repeated.

"Come on, Lynn!" someone called from the crowded front porch.

Lynn didn't say another word before turning away and stumbling back toward the loud party.

I looked to Kyler. "Comes with the territory."

We walked until we reached the quiet end of the street. We stopped at the white picket fence surrounding my lawn. Kyler took it all in. Our small house with decorative shutters, potted flowers by the front steps, the pretty wreath on our front door, and the absence of sofas on the freshly-cut grass. "Now *this* makes sense," he said.

"What does?"

"I didn't take you for a party girl."

"No? Why not?"

He looked over at me and assessed my face. The way his eyes roamed over my features caused something inside me to ignite; something I hadn't known could still exist. "You're better than that."

I laughed. "You have to say that."

"Why?"

"Because you need my help."

He suddenly looked angry. "I don't say anything I don't mean."

I swallowed hard. "Sorry. I just meant…I mean…"

"Nora. I'm not mad," he said, his voice softer. "I just want you to know I'll always give it to you straight."

I nodded once, then walked through the opening in the fence and made my way up the walkway to the front steps. I turned to face Kyler, knowing he'd followed. "Well, this is me," I said, like this was the awkward end of some first date where you don't know if the guy's gonna move in for the kiss so you stall but only long enough to feel him out.

He nodded, though there was indecision in his eyes—uncertainty.

I chewed on my bottom lip, knowing I couldn't just send him away to walk aimlessly all night long. "You wanna come in?"

He blinked, my offer clearly catching him off guard.

"I mean. No pressure. I just didn't want you walking around all night with nowhere to go."

"I appreciate that. But won't your roommate have a problem with a spirit in your house?"

"Oh, she's not home. And, she's used to me talking to spirits."

He exhaled and I could tell he appreciated my offer. "Thank you." He followed me up the front steps and waited while I unlocked the door. He followed me into the living room, his eyes moving from the small Christmas tree set up in front of the picture window with the colorful lights to the red Christmas pillows adding a splash of color to our cream sofa and loveseat. "This is nice."

"Yeah. We got lucky with this one. Last year we were in one of those other houses."

"So, you *were* a party girl."

"Not by choice," I laughed. "You can stay there tonight." I gestured to the sofa.

He looked at it. "Thank you."

"Stop thanking me. It's what I do."

A smirk crawled into his cheek. "Your superpower."

"My superpower," I agreed. "Good night."

"Good night, Nora," he said.

That smooth way my name left his lips made my insides warm, and I so wished a real guy had the same effect. As I turned and headed to my room upstairs, I couldn't shake the butterflies whirling in my belly. A spirit had never made me feel so off-balance, and I realized why. It was a futile endeavor to fall for someone who would disappear without warning. Someone who— as much as they seemed to be—wasn't really there.

CHAPTER 3

"Morning," I said from the doorway between the kitchen and living room.

Kyler lay on the sofa with his hands locked behind his head. "Hey." He kicked his legs down and sat up. "Your roommate never came home."

I smiled. "Did you wait up?"

"I don't exactly sleep," he explained.

I winced. I may have spoken to spirits, but I'd never spent significant time around them. I guess I never considered what they were doing when I wasn't around.

"Aren't you worried about her?" he asked.

"She's a traveling nurse. She's gone for a couple of months at a time. This time she's in California."

"You could've told me that before I paced the floor waiting for her."

"You did not," I challenged.

"I did not," he admitted.

I smiled, realizing he wasn't just a good-looking guy; he also had a great personality and was fun to be around. "I'm gonna shower and then I'll be ready to head to your parents' house. Do we have a plan?"

"You tell me. You do this sort of thing all the time, don't you?"

"Yeah, but I don't usually seek people out. They come to me."

"Oh, right."

"How about you think about it while I'm in the shower, and then we'll strategize on our way there?"

"Deal," he said with a reassuring smile.

"Do you need anything?"

"No. Just some good luck."

I nodded. "No luck needed. I'll talk to them."

* * *

By the time I pulled open my car door, Kyler had already appeared in the passenger seat. I'd never get used to the way spirits traveled. "Tell me about your family," I said once I'd slipped into the driver's seat and started the engine.

"Well, I was their favorite," he said as I backed out of the driveway.

"Why aren't I shocked that you think that?" I said.

"What?" He smiled. "I'm serious."

I drove through town, passing the café and shops, as well as the sidewalks packed with shoppers.

"Okay. Truth?" he asked.

"Yes."

"I'm an only child. So, I kinda had to be their favorite."

I laughed until the truth silenced me. These poor people lost their only child. Hopefully, whatever I was able to tell them would bring them some peace. "I'm an only child too," I admitted.

"Were you spoiled?"

I pursed my lips as I considered it. "A little."

He laughed. "See? You were your parents' favorite, too."

I shrugged, reluctant to unload all my own stuff on him. He *was* the spirit. My responsibility was to help *him*.

"So, what's the plan? Who should I say I am? A friend? Or, do you think being straightforward about what I can do would be better?"

"Oh, definitely say a friend. I'm not so sure they'll let you inside if you start with the medium stuff."

"Would you have believed in the medium stuff if you hadn't experienced it for yourself?"

He paused, his lips twisting in contemplation. "Probably not. It's tough to be open to stuff you can't see."

"Problem is, I've always been able to see. Even if it wasn't with my eyes, I could see in my head. I don't know what it's like not to see."

He reached over and placed his hand on mine.

I pulled mine back as if electrocuted by his touch.

"Jesus! What's wrong?" he asked.

I swerved my car over to the side of the road and threw it into park. "I felt that."

"Felt what?"

"Your touch," I said, my heartbeat thrashing in my chest.

"Is that weird?"

"Extremely. I've never felt a spirit before." I cradled my hand with my other hand, as if it was somehow injured by his touch. "The same way you can just pass through things, my hand passes through spirits."

"What do you think it means?" he asked.

"I have no freaking clue." My mind reeled. This wasn't normal. First, I didn't know he was a spirit when I met him. Now, he can touch me. What the hell was going on? "Can I try something?"

"Yeah, of course."

I lifted my hand slowly, moving it toward his shoulder. Once I placed it against the soft fabric of his black hoodie, I yanked my hand away. "Jesus Christ."

"You're scaring me, Nora."

"Scaring *you*? This has never happened before."

"Well, maybe me being able to see my parents through you might actually work."

I inhaled, needing to remember what I was there for. I was there to bridge the gap between Kyler and his family. I'd have to figure out what the hell was going on with me later. "Right."

I shifted the car back into drive and drove in silence until we reached Kyler's neighborhood. Each home was decked out for Christmas and I realized quickly that Kyler had grown up in a picturesque setting.

"It's that one," he said, pointing at the white colonial decorated with pretty wreaths and red bows on every window.

I parked in front of his house. "It's beautiful."

"My mom loves decorating. I'm surprised she only did the windows."

"I think it looks lovely."

"Yeah, but that's unlike her not to do lights and lawn ornaments."

"She's probably not in the mood given what happened to you," I said.

"Dammit!" He dropped his face into his palms and fell forward. "I'm such a selfish bastard," he growled.

"Why?"

"I haven't even considered what they've been going through."

I reached over and rubbed my hand over his back, still shocked that I could touch him. "Go easy on yourself. You're dealing with a lot."

"That's the problem. I've been so wrapped up in me and my situation that I hadn't thought about how my parents were handling it." He lowered his hands and looked at me. "Maybe that's why I'm still here. Maybe I haven't learned how to move on when I'm so consumed with myself."

"That's not how it works."

"Then how?"

"Once you cross over, any selfish thoughts or transgressions seem to disappear. It wouldn't be the cause of you still being here."

He looked out the window toward his house.

"So, what happens when you go up there? You can't pass through the door?" I asked.

"I've never even been able to get this close. It's like an invisible wall keeps me from this road."

"Well, you made it onto the road. Hopefully, your parents let me in and you can just follow me inside."

He nodded.

I rested my hand on his arm. "Look, I know this isn't easy. But I'll do whatever you need me to do."

"Thanks. I appreciate that."

I opened my door and a cold chill whooshed inside. Goosebumps scampered up my arms as I stepped out.

Kyler appeared at my side. "Let's do this."

I smiled as I closed the door, hoping for his sake it worked. We made our way up the walkway to the front door. A wreath with a big red bow at the top hung on it. I pressed my hand to the door. "Try to get in this way," I said.

He placed his hand beside mine, but it was stopped by the solid door.

"That's okay. Hopefully, you can just follow me inside." I rang the doorbell and the melodic chime echoed inside the home.

Within seconds, the door unlocked. Once it opened, a woman stood there eyeing me while I eyed her. She had shoulder-length blonde hair and the same up-turned lips as Kyler's.

"Mom," he said beside me, the longing to see her etched in the word.

"Hi, Mrs. Fletcher. My name's Nora. I was a friend of Kyler's."

Her eyes narrowed.

"She doesn't believe you," Kyler said, sensing something in his mother's look that I wasn't keen to.

"Then why haven't you been by before?" she asked, suspicion heavy in her tone.

"Oh…I…"

"You what?" she snapped.

"I've been busy?"

She balked. "Everyone wants to see for themselves the stories they've seen online," she said, disdain dripping from her tongue. "It's despicable."

"I've been in Florida," I lied.

"Don't come back here. We've suffered enough." She slammed the door in my face.

"Dammit," Kyler cursed.

"I'm sorry," I said, turning to face him. "She just caught me off guard."

"Try again," he said. "Make her listen to you."

I cocked my head. "Kyler. She's gonna call the police if I push her."

"Then let her," he said.

"I want to help you. I really do. But we need another approach." I noticed movement by the side of the house. I stepped down one of the steps and looked over. A gray-haired woman in light blue scrubs stepped out of a medical van parked in the long driveway. "Who's she?" I asked Kyler.

"I have no idea."

She noticed me staring at her and called over, "Can I help you?"

I stepped off the front steps and approached her. "I'm Nora," I said. "I was a friend of Kyler's."

Sympathy shone in her eyes. "I'm Sue. I can let you in."

"Oh…I…" I glanced at Kyler who shrugged.

Sue watched me as I tried to decide if that was the right move or not. It wasn't like I could just ask Kyler what I should do. Sue checked her watch. "I really need to get in to see Mr. Fletcher."

"What's wrong with my dad?" Kyler asked with fear in his voice.

"Is Mr. Fletcher ill?" I asked her.

Confusion filled her features. "Mr. Fletcher has been in a coma since his accident."

My eyes widened as I looked to Kyler who seemed just as shocked as I was. "I'm alive?" he said, clearly unable to grasp what she'd just told us.

I looked back to Sue. "He's still alive?"

"If you call a coma alive," she said.

Oh. My. God.

"That wasn't in the article?" Kyler asked me.

"I never finished reading it," I said to him, just as awed as he was. "My phone alarm rang, and I needed to lock up the café."

"What?" Sue asked, confused by my mention of things she didn't understand. Why would she understand? *I* didn't understand. I'd been speaking to a spirit who was still alive in that house!

"Jesus Christ," Kyler said, still reeling from the news.

I acknowledged Sue and tried to offer her some version of the truth. "The news article about the accident. I thought Kyler was dead. I saw the word coma and never finished reading it. That's why I didn't realize he was still with us." *That*, and the fact that I'd only ever seen the spirit of a *dead* person. But Kyler *wasn't* dead.

"It's certainly been a difficult year," Sue said.

"Yeah," I agreed, unable to wrap my own head around how all of this was unraveling. "Does Kyler get many visitors?"

"Melanie seems to be the only one who ever stops by these days. Poor girl. I can't imagine having been in that car when…well…when you know," she said.

I nodded.

"Did you want to see him?" Sue asked.

I winced. "I don't think Mrs. Fletcher trusts me since I haven't stopped by before."

Sympathy returned to Sue's eyes. "She hasn't been in a good place since the accident as I'm sure you can imagine."

I nodded.

"If you come back around ten on Monday, Mr. Fletcher will be at work and Mrs. Fletcher will be at her weekly therapist appointment." She smiled as if we shared a secret.

"How about Melanie?"

"She'll be in class. I reckon she wouldn't appreciate a pretty girl like yourself sitting with her boyfriend."

I smiled. "Thank you."

"See you then," she said before making her way inside the house.

I turned to Kyler, but he'd disappeared. I spun around, looking for him by my car, but he wasn't there. I looked down the street first to the right and then left, but he wasn't there. Had he disappeared for good? Had he learned what he needed to learn from me? I'd never seen the spirit of someone who was still alive. Did my ability to see him mean that there was really no hope left for him?

I walked down the driveway toward my car. I opened my door and was about to slip into my seat when I spotted him standing stark still on the side of the house staring into a first-floor window. "Kyler," I whisper-yelled.

He didn't budge.

Now that he was able to get close to his home, he probably didn't want to leave. But could I really leave him there? I sighed and closed my door. I walked along the sidewalk until I reached the far end of their property, then cut a sharp right and speed-walked to Kyler hoping no one saw me. Mrs. Fletcher was definitely going to call the police if she spotted me there. "Hey," I said as I stepped up beside him.

He didn't say a word, just stared into the window. The blinds had been raised so there was an unobstructed view of the room inside. There was a hospital bed in the center of the room with Kyler in it, attached to a ventilator, tubes, an IV, and other machines. An empty chair sat beside his bed.

"Oh," I said, just as shocked to be seeing him that way as he was.

"This is why I'm still here," he said.

"Yeah," I said, though he may not have been asking.

"Do you think it means I'm really dead and they just don't know it?" he asked.

"That machine right there, the one showing your heart rate, means part of you is still alive."

"Then why am I here *and* there?"

"I have no idea."

"Maybe I need to enter my body. Isn't that how it's done in the movies?" He reached out his hand and placed it against the window. The glass stopped it. "Fuuuuuck. What do I do now? Just hang out here until I die?"

My eyes shot around. A neighbor climbed on a ladder hanging Christmas lights two houses down. It was just a matter of time before he became suspicious of me staring into the Fletchers' window. "I need to go before someone sees me," I said to Kyler. "You stay."

He turned to me and wrapped his arms around me. I stilled, surprised by the gesture *and* the feel of him holding me so closely. His arms were safe and strong— and not really real. But, if I was being honest, they were the most real thing I'd felt from a guy in a long time.

"Thank you, Nora. I never would've known if you didn't bring me here." He released me and stepped back, burying his hands in his pockets.

"I'll be back on Monday. If you're unable to get in between now and then, hopefully, you'll be able to get inside with me."

He nodded.

"I'll see ya then," I said before turning and heading toward my car. With each step, a pit grew in my stomach. I'd never helped someone like this. I'd relayed messages, but I'd never been so involved—so invested—in their life.

And, never before had a spirit been alive.

CHAPTER 4

"I can't believe it."

"It was crazy," I said to Izzy on speakerphone. The fire in the fireplace crackled as I pulled the throw blanket around me, trying to get warm as I filled Izzy in on Kyler.

"Are you gonna go there on Monday?" Izzy asked.

"I have to. He needs to try to get inside."

"What's he look like?"

A vision of him played in my mind's eye. His green eyes mirrored tropical waters. His lips looked like he was grinning about something only he knew. His strong arms still felt as if they'd branded my skin.

"Your silence speaks volumes," Izzy said, interrupting my thoughts. "What's his name? I'm looking him up."

"Kyler Fletcher."

She was quiet for a minute and then she said, "Holy shit."

"Yeah."

She laughed. "Yeah."

There was a knock on my door.

"What was that?" she asked.

"Someone's here," I whispered.

"It's almost midnight," she said loudly. "Who is it?"

"*Shhhh,*" I whispered as I pulled off my blanket.

"Well? Who is it?" she repeated.

"*Shhhh*," I whispered as I crept over to the window and peeked out. Kyler stood on my front steps. "It's him."

"Well, go let him in. *Wait*. Can't he walk through walls?"

Realizing what he was doing, I smiled. He was being respectful by not barging in on me. "I'll call you later." I didn't give her time to respond before I disconnected the call and opened the door.

"How long were you gonna make me wait out here?" he asked.

"Don't pretend you can feel the cold."

A soft chuckle slipped past his lips.

"Thanks for respecting my privacy," I said, moving to the side to let him in.

He moved by me into my living room.

I closed the door and locked it. "You okay?" I asked as I turned to face him.

"You mean after finding out I've been in a coma for a year?"

I winced. "I'm so sorry. That was a stupid question."

"I'm joking, Nora," he said as he sat down on my sofa where he'd slept the night before. "You can relax."

I released a silent breath. "Did you see your dad? Or Melanie?"

"I saw my dad for just a minute. I could tell he didn't like being in that room with what's left of me. And Melanie came for a couple of hours. But most of the time she was on her phone. I guess she just likes being there with me."

"Do you remember her now?" I asked, sitting down on the arm of the loveseat.

"I remember her because we went to high school together. But when I looked at her, I didn't feel anything. Like, when I see my parents, I want to go hug them and be near them and talk to them. I want them to see me. But when I see her, I don't. Does that make sense?"

"The brain is a funny thing. Especially, after you've been through what you've been through. You'll remember everything when you're meant to."

He didn't respond, growing quiet.

The fire crackled, emphasizing the silence that crept between us.

I checked my phone and found four texts from Izzy.

Did he come in?

What did he want?

Is he still there?

Helloooooo?

I smiled.

"Boyfriend?" Kyler asked.

I shook my head. "No. They're too much trouble."

He laughed. "You're probably right."

"Just my roommate," I explained as I shot off a text responding to all four of her texts. **Yes. Idk. Yes. Goodbye.**

"Would you mind if I stayed again?" Kyler asked, pulling my attention away from my phone.

Ohhhh. That's why he came back. "Sure."

He looked relieved.

I moved from the arm of the loveseat down onto the seat cushion.

"Can I ask you something?" he said.

I placed my phone down beside me, giving him my full attention. "Sure."

"When did you see your first spirit?" he asked.

I grabbed the throw blanket from the back of the loveseat. "I've been hearing voices and having visions in my mind since I was five, but I didn't see a spirit until I was nine."

"Was it scary?"

I shook my head. "It was my dad."

"Jesus, Nora. I'm sorry. I didn't know you lost your dad."

"How would you know?" I asked, wrapping the blanket around my shoulders.

"Would you mind me asking what happened?"

I pulled the blanket tighter around me. "He'd been really sick with cancer. It was hard watching him turn into a shell of himself. So, when the time came, I told him it was okay to go because I'd see him again one day. And then, he let go."

"And you saw him again," Kyler said.

I nodded.

"Wow."

"Yeah. He still appears to me from time to time. But, he gives me space and respects my privacy."

"That's really cool."

"I guess. But I'd rather have the real thing any day."

Kyler was quiet, and I worried I may have divulged too much. I picked up my phone, trying to occupy the silence. Izzy had sent me back three angry-face emojis.

"Why didn't you know I was a spirit right away?" Kyler asked.

"Spirits usually possess a very subtle glow. When you walked into the café, I must've been tired or something and missed it," I lied, knowing full well I'd been distracted by his good looks.

He smiled a knowing smile.

"Did you know that anyone can learn to do what I do and communicate with the other side?" I asked, but he just shook his head. "Most people can learn to do it. It's all about getting extremely relaxed and being open to it."

"That's kinda crazy," he said.

I shrugged. It was my normal, so I didn't really know any different. "Did you expect me to be a little old lady with a crystal ball when you came to the café?"

He grinned. "Not sure. But I was happily surprised."

Embarrassed by his words, my eyes avoided his.

"Does that make you uncomfortable?" he asked.

I met his gaze. Yes. "No."

"Liar," he said with a grin.

"Spirit," replied with my own. "You know, you're kind of easy to talk to."

"Yeah?" he asked surprised. "You should've met me as a kid. You wouldn't be saying that."

"Why? What were you like?"

He laughed. "A terror. You know I'm an only child. So, my parents had to know I'd end up that way if I got everything I wanted."

I laughed. "Did you play sports? I picture you being an athlete."

"Football. I played in college too. I wasn't going to the pros or anything, but I was fast so I scored a lot."

"I bet you did," I smirked.

"Oh, I saw what you did there."

"Am I wrong?" I challenged.

"Not exactly."

"I knew it," I said.

"Oh, you did, huh?"

I shrugged as I readjusted my blanket around me.

He pegged me with narrowed eyes. "What did the last guy you dated do to you to make you swear off guys?"

"Who said I've sworn off guys?"

"You said they're all trouble. Same thing."

I scoffed, surprised he picked up on that. "He cheated with someone I thought was a friend."

"Harsh," he said. "How'd you find out?"

"You sure you wanna hear? It's a pretty pathetic story."

"Tell me," he urged.

I exhaled a long breath. "Izzy, Zoe, and I were supposed to go shopping. Zoe backed out last minute to take her mom to the doctor, so Izzy and I decided to go to the beach instead. I walked up to the boardwalk to get food, and boom. Zoe was there kissing my boyfriend."

"What'd you do?"

"Told *her* we were done and punched *him* in the face."

Kyler's mouth parted. "No way?"

"Way. And it hurt." I looked down at my hand. "My knuckles were swollen for a week."

"You're a badass," he said.

"Not really. I was just pissed."

"Did it make you feel better?" he asked.

I considered his question and all the pain I'd suffered due to their betrayal. Then, I shook my head. "They made it hard to trust people. I trusted *them* and they stabbed me in the back. Not to mention, they ruined the beach for me. And I really loved the beach."

"I'm sorry they did that to you. They suck."

"I can't really complain about my life right now, can I?" I said, knowing his life was currently in shambles.

"Don't do that. Our lives can all suck. They just suck in different ways."

"That's optimistic," I teased.

"I'm all about spreading the optimism over here," he laughed.

Once his laughter subsided and was replaced with the crackling from the fireplace, I said, "Seriously, what sucks for you—and don't say the obvious being caught between two worlds thing?"

"Not eating."

"That would suck," I said, forgetting that he couldn't eat anymore. "What do you miss most?"

"Peanut butter," he said without even thinking about it.

"Of everything out there—pizza, burgers, ice cream—you miss peanut butter?"

"Yup, and I'm not even sorry about it."

I laughed. "What are you happy you'll never have to eat again?"

"Mushrooms and onions. I hate them."

I laughed. "Why?"

"Their texture." He shivered at the thought. "*Yuuuckk*"

I yawned.

"Am I boring you?" he asked.

"Not at all. I'm just tired."

He nodded his understanding.

"I should probably get to bed." I shed the blanket and stood up. "Want me to leave the television on for you?"

"Can you put on *The Hangover*?" he asked.

"That's such a guy movie."

He shrugged offhandedly. "I'm a guy."

He certainly was.

I grabbed the remote and streamed the movie for him. The credits appeared on the screen. "All set?"

He stared across the space between us for a long beat. "Thanks, Nora."

"It's just a movie," I said, knowing that's not what he meant. But I hated the fact that he felt like he constantly needed to thank me for helping him.

He smirked, realizing *exactly* what I was doing. *Damn spirit.* "Good night."

"Night," I said before making my way to my room and flopping down on my bed.

I'd lied to Kyler.

There was no way I was getting any sleep, especially with him under my roof. I hadn't, however, lied about getting cheated on. That broke my heart in ways I didn't think I'd be able to come back from. Nor, did I think I'd ever feel anything ever again. But here I was, attracted to the guy in my living room. The semi-*dead* guy in my living room. I knew it was crazy. I knew he was on the verge of crossing over to the other side. But his presence brought light back into my life. And I liked it more than I had any right to.

CHAPTER 5

"Hey," Kyler said, "Nice jammies."

I looked down at my plaid cotton pajamas. "Thanks."

"What are we up to today?" he asked.

"*We?*"

He laughed. "It's not like I have other plans."

"Who said I'm even getting out of my pajamas today? I *am* a college girl on winter break."

"Why aren't you going home?" he asked.

"This is my home."

"What about your mom?" he asked.

"She's a traveling nurse. She got Izzy into it. She'll be home on Christmas morning so I'm either alone at her condo or alone here."

"But you're not alone here," he said. "You've got me."

I tipped my head, appreciating him for that.

"Did you get your mom a gift yet? I bet you could pick her up something today."

"Come to think of it," I said, "I do need to pick up a gift."

"Great. It's a date."

I pushed back the butterflies trying to take flight in

my stomach. It was *not* a date. "Let me just get showered and I'll be ready to go."

"I'm not going anywhere," he assured me.

But he was. It was just a matter of when.

* * *

"So, you're still up for going to my house tomorrow?" Kyler asked as we walked down the sidewalk after stopping at a couple of shops.

I nodded, trying to use as few words as possible so I didn't draw attention to me talking to myself.

"Do you think it's gonna work? Me getting into the house?" he asked.

I shrugged as a girl and her mother walked directly at us, not giving up their space on the sidewalk. I moved to the side, thinking Kyler would too, but he kept walking and they passed right through him like he was nothing more than air. I gasped, stopping in my tracks. "Why didn't they walk into you?" I whispered, not even waiting for them to be out of earshot.

"I don't know."

"Can you control it?"

"I have no idea," he said. "Sometimes, maybe."

"Good to know," I said as we were about to pass the café. "Mind if I stop in?"

"Not at all."

As soon as the bell's jingle announced our arrival inside the café, Daci called, "Here on your day off?"

"What can I say? The hot chocolate is to die for." I instantly regretted my choice of words. "Sorry," I whispered to Kyler.

He laughed.

"Whip cream?" she asked as we approached the counter during what appeared to be a lull in customers.

"Obviously."

She spun away from me and went to work on my drink. "Any good stories?" she asked, glancing over her shoulder at me.

"Tell her about the hot guy who's been sleeping over at your house," Kyler said. "You know she wants to know."

"Pretty boring," I told her.

Kyler laughed, knowing the intentional omission was intended for him.

"Come on," she whined. "You're killing me. I need to live vicariously through you, and you're giving me nothing."

"As soon as something interesting happens, you'll be the first to know."

She turned toward me and handed me my drink. "Why do I get the feeling that you're not telling me something?"

I dodged her inquiry with a smile. "Thanks, Daci."

She hmphed.

I laughed. "See you tomorrow."

"Why is she so invested in your life?" Kyler asked as we walked back outside.

"She misses college," I said.

"Yeah. I do too," he said as we walked along the sidewalk.

"You can always come to my classes with me next semester if you miss it that much."

"I don't miss *that* part of it."

We walked into a candle shop and I lifted candle after candle to my nose, but despite the sweet fragrances of many, I was always drawn to vanilla.

"So, your boss understands your gift?" Kyler asked.

"Yeah. During freshman year I was in the café with Izzy and this spirit kept following Daci around. I finally had to pull her aside and tell her."

"Did she believe you?" he asked.

"At first, she looked at me like I was crazy, but once I told her everything her spirit was saying, she broke into full-blown tears and believed every word."

"Who was the spirit?"

"A close friend of hers. Daci held a lot of pain over her death and the spirit wanted to help her heal. Ever since then, she's been one of my biggest supporters."

"So, why not tell her about me?" he asked with a raised brow.

"Do you really want me to?"

"Not if you don't want to," he said. "How'd your ex feel about your gift?"

"He acted like it didn't happen. Like a dirty secret I should keep hidden. That's why I keep a lot of my interactions to myself."

"It sucks that you feel like you can't be open with everyone," he said, likely not realizing how spot-on he was. "So, what are you hoping to get for Christmas?" he asked, changing the subject because he probably sensed my mood change.

I shrugged. "I don't really need anything." But that was another lie. I needed love. Better yet, I needed to *be* loved.

CHAPTER 6

"You seem nervous," Kyler said as we drove to his house the next day.

I flipped down my visor to block the morning sun as we turned into his neighborhood. "Nope," I said, unsure what the clawing sensation in my chest was about.

"Do you think I'll disappear once I meet myself?" he asked.

My eyes shot to his. "Do *you* think you'll disappear?"

"I hope not."

"If that were going to happen, you wouldn't be having such a hard time getting into your house."

"Maybe you're right," he said. "Would you miss me if I disappeared?"

I glanced over at him. "Maybe a little."

He laughed. "I knew you liked me."

I couldn't imagine any girl *not* liking him.

"Sue's van's here," he said, quickly sitting up straighter in his seat as we pulled to a stop in front of his house.

I inhaled a deep breath as my hands gripped the steering wheel, my knuckles turning white. *Was* I nervous he'd disappear? Or, was I more worried about how badly this could go?

He reached over and placed his hand on mine. "You got this."

I tried to ignore the warmth spreading through my hand and up my arm. His touch was so damn real and that notion scared the hell out of me because I might just start to believe it. I slipped my hand away and switched off the engine. It was go time. "Let's do this." I pushed open my door and stepped out. I didn't hear Kyler's door slam shut, probably because he didn't have to open it to pass through it before meeting me in the front of the car. I wrapped my scarf around my neck as we made our way up the driveway and to the side of the house. I knocked on the side door and waited, listening for a voice or footsteps. "Do you think we should've gone to the front door? Do you think she remembers me? Do you think she told your mom? Do you think she forgot I'm coming?"

Kyler reached over and rubbed a reassuring hand over my back. "You're rambling."

"Am not," I snapped, knowing I was totally rambling.

"She'll remember you."

The door unlocked and then opened. Sue smiled when she found me standing there. "You came back?" she said.

"Of course." I stepped inside with Kyler on my heels.

"I'm in," he said, relief in his voice.

"Thank God," I said.

"What?" Sue asked.

"Thank God you remember me," I explained.

"Of course," she said.

As I followed Sue through the kitchen, I glanced to my side to be sure Kyler was still with me. He looked all around, taking in the home he'd grown up in as we trailed Sue down a hallway to the small bedroom at the far end of the first floor. She stopped in the doorway causing me to stop.

"Mrs. Fletcher will be home around eleven-thirty, so you might want to leave before then so you don't run into her."

"No problem. Thanks for letting me visit."

She smiled, stepping aside so I could enter the room. I moved past her and stopped at the side of the hospital bed. Sue's footsteps retreated down the hallway as I stared down at Kyler. He lay under the sheets with his arms at his sides and his eyes closed. If I didn't know any better, I would've thought he was asleep—save the ventilator tube in his mouth and the monotonous clicking of the machine keeping him alive.

"Jesus Christ," Kyler said from beside me.

I jumped, almost forgetting there were two of them.

"I look like shit," he observed.

I lowered myself into the empty chair beside the bed, pushed myself to the edge of it, and lifted my hand to his cheek. "Can you feel me?" I asked, though anyone watching would've thought I was talking to the Kyler in the bed.

"No," he said from beside me.

"Try to touch yourself," I said.

He stepped up to the bed and leaned down, slowly moving his hand toward his arm. He stopped mere inches from his body.

"What's wrong?"

"I can't get any closer," he said, struggling to touch his other self.

I grabbed his wrist and tried to pull it closer for him, but something invisible—not to mention inexplicably solid—stopped it from moving any further. "I guess jumping into your body is out of the question," I said as I released his wrist.

"I guess so," he conceded.

"I'm sorry," I said, knowing it was an inadequate thing to say.

"Not your fault," he assured me.

I reached under the sheet and covered his hand with mine. Then, I reached over and held his hand beside me. If he couldn't touch his own body, I'd somehow find a way to connect them.

"Am I cold?" he asked.

"No. You feel the same," I said, brushing my thumbs over the backs of both of his hands.

A long silence passed as we both stared at Kyler in the bed.

"This isn't my room," he finally said, breaking the silence. "Mine's upstairs."

"Maybe they wanted you closer to them during the day," I offered.

He released my hand, leaving it bereft of his warmth. "I'm gonna head upstairs and see if they changed anything." And though he said it like it was no big deal, I could sense he didn't like seeing himself lifeless and hollow. I didn't blame him.

Once he disappeared from the room, I spoke to his other self, wondering if I could somehow break through to him. "You in there?" I asked, not really expecting a response. "Maybe you could just wake up and all of this could be over. I know he'd appreciate it." I paused, but again there was no response. I glanced at the screen on the machine beside him. His heart rate was steady. That had to mean there was still hope, right? "Where have you gone? You've gotta be in there somewhere…" I stared at the tube in his mouth and the rise and fall of his chest, hating that this was what had become of such a fun-loving guy. "I would've loved to know you before your accident. I know you would've been the center of attention—at least all the girls would've been watching you even if you didn't realize it…"

"Who are *you*?" a voice demanded from the doorway.

I glanced over my shoulder.

A girl with long blonde hair and perfect makeup glared at me.

"Oh…I…"

She walked in and her eyes shot to my hand holding Kyler's under the sheet.

I slipped my hand free and fixed the sheet, trying to make the gesture look innocent.

"I asked you a question," she clipped.

"I'm Nora. A friend of Kyler's." I stood from the chair.

She was a few inches shorter than me and swiftly slid into my newly vacated seat. "I know all of his friends," she said, her eyes drifting over my jeans and hoodie. "How do you know him?"

I swallowed. "School."

Her eyes narrowed, not buying my story. "He never mentioned you," she said as she slid her own hand under the sheet so she could hold his hand.

"I didn't catch your name."

"Melanie."

I shook my head. "Can't say he ever mentioned you either."

Anger grabbed hold of her features, her face growing taut and on the verge of bursting. "Well, I'm here now. You can run along." Her gaze moved from mine to Kyler in bed.

"Ugh, she's back?" Kyler said as he returned to the room.

I glanced to him in the doorway.

"Ask her about the accident. Maybe it'll help me remember," he said.

"You were in the car that night?" I said as she continued to stare at him.

"So?" she said.

"How did you manage to get out unscathed?"

"Unscathed?!" Her eyes cut to mine, cold and unabashed. "You call having my boyfriend in a coma unscathed?"

"Ask where we were going," Kyler said as he crossed his arms and stared at her.

"Where were you going that night?" I asked.

"We were coming back from a party," she said, her eyes moving back to him.

"And, he just lost control of the car?" I asked.

"It was dark and icy," she mumbled.

"Ask whose party we were at," he urged.

"Whose party?" I asked.

"No one you'd know," she said.

"She's such a bitch," he said. "I can't believe I dated her."

"Yup," I agreed.

"What?" she snapped.

"You're right. I probably wouldn't know them. We had our own friends at school so he didn't really talk about anyone here," I lied.

"We've known each other since eighth grade and we've been together since last summer," she said. "He never mentioned me?"

"Sorry," I said.

Her jaw clenched, ticking wildly.

"Was he drunk?" I asked.

"No," her tone was low and menacing.

"Let's go," Kyler said. "You're just pissing her off and it's pissing me off that I can't remember."

"Well, I should probably leave you two alone," I said moving toward the door.

"No need to come back," she muttered. "He's got me."

I said nothing as I walked out.

"She was pleasant," I mumbled as we made our way toward the kitchen.

"A dream," he agreed.

"I'm so sorry," Sue said as we found her in the kitchen. "I didn't realize she'd be by."

"No problem," I said. "Thanks for letting me sit with him."

"How'd it go?"

"It was nice seeing him."

She gave me a sad smile.

"Any idea if he'll wake up?" I asked.

"The world works in mysterious ways," she said. "You just never know in cases like these."

"I'll keep praying for him," I assured her.

"He needs all the prayers he can get."

Kyler looked at me and something about the sadness in his eyes told me he knew—after seeing himself—that the odds of him ever waking up were not very good.

CHAPTER 7

"Trish," I called, placing a mocha latte on the counter. Christmas music played in the background as a woman maneuvered through the groups of people waiting for their orders.

"What time's your reading today?" Daci asked.

I spun around and grabbed the coffee she just made. "Four."

"Do you need to meditate first?"

I swiped the caramel bottle and squirted a heart-shaped design on the top of the frothed milk in the cup. "Yeah, but only for a few minutes. I've already been getting visions of her loved ones." I placed the cup down on the counter. "Steve," I called as the man who ordered the drink made his way over to grab it.

"Hi, Nora."

I spun around, my eyes widening on Zoe. Her red hair was curled and shorter than it had been the last time I'd seen her.

Daci stepped up beside me, glaring at Zoe. "We're out of everything. You should leave."

"I think Nora can speak for herself," Zoe said with her chin lifted in bravado.

"You should leave," I said before addressing the next woman in line. "May I help you?"

Zoe pushed her way in front of the woman. "You have to talk to me sometime, Nora."

"I'm surprised you're here and not off stealing someone else's boyfriend," I said.

"Are you really gonna throw away three years of friendship?"

I scoffed. "I didn't throw it away. *You* did."

"Rick and I aren't together anymore," she said.

"I don't care."

Her gaze lowered. "I guess once a cheater always a cheater."

I nearly choked on my own laughter. "Please tell me you're not here thinking I'm going to feel sorry for you."

Her eyes lifted to mine. "I just thought you'd want to know."

"Well, you're wrong."

I looked around her to the woman she cut in line. "May I help you?"

"Hot chocolate with skim milk and a slice of lemon pie," the woman said around Zoe's back.

I turned to the hot chocolate machine and grabbed a mug, mixing in skim milk and chocolate syrup as it poured.

"Is Izzy home yet?" Zoe asked.

I didn't turn back to her. "You have her number."

"She won't return my texts," she admitted.

I placed the hot chocolate on the counter. "I guess she doesn't want a backstabber as a friend either."

She buried her hands in her coat pockets. "I deserve that."

I moved to the display case with the lemon pie and placed a piece on a dish before cashing the woman out. She took her order and left, but Zoe didn't go.

"I miss you," Zoe persisted.

I stared at her feeling absolutely nothing. Not sadness. Not hate. Nothing.

Reading the indifference in my eyes, she said. "I guess I just thought you'd hear me out if I came here."

"I heard you. Now, please don't come back here," I said, impressed that her plea didn't stir the least bit of emotion in me. She destroyed our friendship. Not me.

She blinked back tears before turning and walking out of the café.

I stood frozen to my spot for a long moment, unsure why she thought I'd care about their breakup.

"You okay?" Daci asked.

I turned to look at her standing nearby. "Yeah. But can I just have a minute?"

"Of course," she said. "Julie should be here soon anyway."

"Thanks," I said before moving into the back room.

I squatted with my back to the brick wall, covering my face with my hands. I just needed a moment to regroup. I'd been able to avoid Zoe all semester. Did she really think I'd be happy they broke up, like I'd been waiting for it to happen so I could have him back? Didn't she know I thought they deserved each other and wanted nothing to do with either one of them ever again?

"Nora?"

I dropped my hands and looked up. Kyler moved toward me with effortless swagger. I blinked hard. Zoe may not have been a welcome sight, but *he* certainly was.

"Are you okay?" he asked.

I nodded as I stood up, surprised to even see him there. He hadn't said a single word on the drive home from his parents' house yesterday. And, once we returned to my house, he told me he was going for a walk but never returned.

"What are you doing back here?" he asked, a tinge of concern in his voice.

"Just taking a minute," I said, my eyes drifting over his hoodie and jeans. "I'm glad to see you're okay."

Kyler leaned beside me against the brick wall. "*Okay* is a subjective thing given my situation."

"What are you doing here?" I asked. "Did you need something?"

"I just wanted to see you."

My stomach flip-flopped. "Yeah?"

He nodded. "I wanted to thank you for bringing me yesterday."

I sighed, stupidly thinking he'd meant something else. But, I steeled my features and acted unfazed. "I didn't really have a choice. You would've haunted me until I did."

He laughed, but his eyes flashed down. "I'm sorry I flaked on you."

"You didn't flake on me," I said.

"It was a lot." His eyes cut sidelong to me. "And I didn't know what to do with it."

"I get it," I assured him, knowing how overwhelmed he must've felt after seeing himself in that state.

"Do you get it? Because I feel like I'm all alone in this," he said.

My eyes widened. "How can you say that when you've got me?"

"I don't have you," he said, his pained eyes avoiding mine again. "I haven't even given you a choice."

I cocked my head. "I don't do anything I don't want to do. If I wanted you to leave me alone, I wouldn't allow you in."

"I really need you, Nora."

"You've got me," I assured him.

"I'm scared."

A fissure cracked in my heart. "I'm here for you. We're in this together."

His eyes locked on mine. "Together?"

I nodded and electricity crackled between us. Could he feel it, too? "Together."

"Nora?"

My head twisted toward the doorway.

Julie stood in the doorway, her pink braids hanging on her shoulders and her brows furrowed. "What are you doing?" she asked.

"Oh…" I said, stepping away from the wall. "Nothing." It wasn't like she didn't know I could speak to spirits. But, striking up a bond with one was a whole other level of crazy. "I'll be right out."

Julie ducked back out front leaving Kyler and me alone once again.

I turned back to him. "I should probably get back out there."

He nodded. "I'll walk you home at the end of your shift."

"I have a reading, so I won't be ready to head out until five," I explained.

"That's fine. It's not like I have other plans."

I laughed, though I knew his situation was far from funny. "I'll see you later." I moved to the doorway and headed back out front, suddenly eager for both my shift and reading to be over.

CHAPTER 8

"That was really cool what you did back there," Kyler said as we walked through town.

I glanced around, making sure no one noticed me talking to myself. "I talk to *you*, don't I?"

"Yeah, but you were able to tell her everything her mother wanted her to know. Did you see the way she was crying?"

"Yeah. That's what happens."

His hand brushed mine, and a shiver rushed up my arm. "Every time?"

"Well, yeah. It's hard to hear that your loved one is so close but you can't see them," I explained.

"Why can only some people see spirits?"

"I told you. Everyone has the ability. They just need to be open to it and hone their skills."

He buried his hands in his hoodie pocket, and I could sense there was something he wanted to say. "Do you think you could do a reading for my mom?" he asked.

"She'd have to be willing to let me, and right now she doesn't trust me," I said.

"But maybe if you tell her about me, she'll..."

"She'll what?"

"Realize I'm still here," he said.

The notion hung heavy in the night.

Was he really still there?

* * *

After showering and slipping on my pajamas, I cooked up a cup of noodles and joined Kyler in the living room. I sat on the loveseat, crossing my legs beneath me. "I'd offer you some, but you know," I said.

"Appreciate the thought," he said from the sofa.

I took a bite, careful not to dribble the broth down my chin.

"The redhead in the café today—"

"You saw that?" I asked.

"Yeah. You were a total badass sending her away like you did. That was the friend you mentioned?" he asked.

"Ex-friend," I clarified. "And, apparently, she and my ex just broke up."

"Who cares? He's a prick."

I laughed. "True story."

"So, why'd she show up at the café?"

"She's lost her ever-loving mind?" I shrugged. "I don't usually hold grudges, but what they did was unforgivable. And to think I almost gave up my virgin—" I froze, realizing what I'd just admitted. I wanted to facepalm right there and then. "I know what you're thinking."

"You may be a medium, but you have no idea what I'm thinking," he assured me.

"Of course, I do. You're thinking it's obvious why he cheated. I made him wait. I wouldn't give it up. It was all my fault."

"Whoa. Hold up. Yes, I'm surprised you're a virgin because you're hot as hell and cool as shit. But I'd never say it was your fault. He knew the score. If he was tired of waiting for you, he should've broken up with you. Not fucked around on you."

"We were together a year."

"So?"

"So, most guys wouldn't wait that long," I said.

"He didn't wait that long," he said. "Please don't tell me you've been beating yourself up over this."

I shrugged. "Not beating myself up, just aware of his reason."

"The only reason he cheated was because he was horny, and your friend—and whoever else he cheated with—gave it up. *You* didn't make him cheat."

I stared into my cup of noodles to avoid eye contact. I felt vulnerable and I didn't know what to do with that.

"Can I ask you something?" he said.

I nodded.

"Why didn't you sleep with him?"

I swallowed around the sudden lump in my throat. "I don't know."

"I don't believe that," he said.

"I know everyone sleeps around, but for me, it's a big decision. I know it sounds lame, but the first guy I'm with needs to be someone special."

"It doesn't sound lame. I guess I'm just wondering why you stayed with a guy for a year but didn't think he was special," he said.

I mixed the noodles in my cup while pondering his words. I thought I loved Rick. I thought he was eventually going to be endgame for me. But maybe I knew down deep that he wasn't the one. Maybe I questioned if I could see a future with him.

"You wouldn't have been able to resist me if we were together," Kyler said, easing the awkwardness in the room.

Laughter burst out of me. "You don't think so?"

"I know so," he said with a huge smile that caused dimples to pucker into his cheeks. "I would've lit candles and played soft music."

"You would've set the mood?" I asked.

He nodded slowly. "And we would've danced across my parents' basement like we were at our prom."

"Your parents' basement?"

"It's where I took all the girls in high school."

I placed my cup of noodles down on the coffee table and threw a pillow at him, hitting him in the head.

"What was that for?" he asked.

"You're ridiculous."

"That's not what the girls used to say," he assured me.

I rolled my eyes.

"You doubt me?"

"Yes," I said.

A devilish glint shone in his eyes as he pushed himself off my sofa and moved to the loveseat, sitting down beside me. The cushion beneath me bowed, telling me—despite what I knew to be the truth—that he was very much there. I couldn't tear my eyes away from his, having no idea what he was doing. "I don't like being doubted," he said, the rasp in his voice sending flutters to my belly.

"I was kidding," I said, though a nervous quiver weakened that assertion.

He lifted his hands to my face, cupping my cheeks gently. "Well, I'm not." He inched closer to my lips. "And I think you've been missing out."

My eyes dropped to his lips, all shiny and turned up in the corners. "On what?" I whispered.

"On what someone special feels like," he whispered before closing the distance between us and pressing his lips to mine, firm and assured. Before I could consider what was happening, his tongue swept across the seam of my lips. Goosebumps scampered up my arms as I gave in, my lips parting and my tongue meeting his. A victorious sigh rumbled in the back of his throat before we went all in, our tongues twining and melding and fighting for control. This was happening. This was freaking happening with a spirit and I didn't want it to end. I wanted to savor how it felt. Savor how he felt. Savor the notion that I could feel anything resembling desire again.

Kyler pulled away first, his hands dropping from my face and his chest heaving. His wild eyes were locked on mine.

"Ummm," I began, my pulse slamming hard against my skin.

He chuckled. "I told you you've been missing out."

My eyes flashed away, unable to look at his hypnotizing green eyes in such close proximity. So many thoughts rushed through my mind. How was it even possible that I could touch him—let alone kiss him? This was unheard of. This wasn't normal. This shouldn't have felt so right. I needed to be the rational one. I needed to stop acting like this was any other guy.

"What are you thinking?" he asked.

I shook my head.

"Nora?" He lifted my chin with his thumb so I had no other option but to look him in the eyes. "Talk to me."

"We shouldn't be able to do that," I said.

"Why not?" he asked, almost hurt by my words.

I shook my head, the words not coming out right. "No, I mean, we shouldn't even be able to touch the way we do. So, kissing is definitely something else."

"Otherworldly?" he asked with a panty-melting smirk.

I rolled my eyes. "You know how to kiss. Am I ever gonna live it down?"

"Not sure," he said, climbing off the loveseat and returning to the sofa.

The spot beside me suddenly felt empty. Why had he moved away? Had he really only been trying to show me what I was missing?

I picked up my cup of noodles, needing something to do with my hands.

"I'd like to go to the bridge," he said.

My shoulders sank. Out of all the things I'd hoped he'd say, him changing the subject—and distancing himself from me—wasn't one of them.

"I think I'll remember something about that night if I go there," he continued.

"Yeah. Of course," I said, steeling my features like a pro. "Whatever you need."

He stared across the space between us. He wanted to say something. I could see it in the way his eyes creased in the corners. But I really didn't want to hear that he felt bad for the poor virgin. That he pitied the girl who'd been cheated on. That he owed me for helping him.

Before tears caused my façade to crack, I placed my noodles down and pushed myself to my feet. "I'm gonna head to bed."

"Oh," he said as if confused by my quick exit.

"I'll see you in the morning and get you to the bridge."

He nodded.

I turned and moved toward the stairs wishing I didn't feel so let down by the turn of events. Wishing I hadn't hoped the kiss meant anything more than it did. I needed to see it for what it was. Him making a point that I was missing out on living.

"Nora?"

I stopped but couldn't bring myself to turn around.

"Thank you."

I released a silent breath, wishing he'd said anything other than that. "Any time." I couldn't escape that room fast enough.

I closed myself in my room and flopped down on my bed, wishing my life wasn't as screwed up as it currently was. And, wishing I wasn't so confused by a kiss that surpassed all others.

CHAPTER 9

The afternoon sun shone down on Kyler and me as we stared over the guardrail, leaning on the new section that must have replaced the broken part from the accident.

"I've never stood on this bridge before," Kyler said as he gazed down at the river flowing thirty feet below. "I've driven over it hundreds of times, but I never realized how deep the water below it is."

"You saved her," I assured him, knowing so many thoughts must have been running through his mind.

"Yeah, I'm a real hero," he said somberly.

"He *is* a hero," a voice beside me said.

I looked to my right. The spirit of an older woman stared down at the water below.

"Kyler? Did your gram pass?"

His eyes cut to mine. "One of them. Why?"

"I think she's standing next to me," I explained.

"Jesus Christ," he said, looking to my left and right. "Why can't I see her?"

I looked at the woman who I now realized resembled Kyler, especially those Fletcher lips. "Why can't he see you?" I asked her.

"Because he's still alive," she said.

"What'd she say?" he asked.

"Because you're still alive," I told him before looking back to her. "Were you there the night it happened? He has a lot of unanswered questions."

She nodded and my heart stammered. "I arrived after the accident. I saw him unbuckle the girl and push her out of the car even though his seatbelt was stuck."

An ache twisted in my heart hearing the firsthand account.

"Was she?" he asked.

"She said you pushed Melanie out of the car but your seatbelt was stuck."

"He was so brave," his grandmother continued. "He tried not to panic, but he was running out of air. He did what he needed to do to save the girl. I wanted to help. Wanted to somehow get the seatbelt unstuck for him, but that's beyond my capabilities," she said regrettably.

"What's she saying?" he asked.

"You were brave. You didn't panic, even when you couldn't breathe." A tear trailed down my cheek, the idea of what he went through burning away at my eyes.

"Hey," he moved to me, using his thumb to wipe my tears. "I'm right here."

I nodded. "It's just hard to hear what you went through."

"If it's any consolation, I don't remember any of it."

"Tell him I love him," his grandmother said.

"She loves you," I said. "Your gram."

"I love her too," he said, though his eyes were on mine.

"Tell him I'll be there when he decides to cross over. It's not a scary place."

I chewed on my bottom lip.

"What?" he asked, reading my look.

"She said she'll be waiting for you when you're ready to cross over."

"And what if I'm not ready?" he asked.

I glanced to her. Her lips twisted with sadness as if she knew how this all ended.

"What'd she say?" he asked.

"She didn't say anything," I explained.

He spun away from me, burying his hands in his pockets, as he stepped around the guardrail and descended the hill to the river. My instinct was to follow after him to give him the support and comfort he needed, but I also knew he needed something more than support and comfort. He needed time.

"Thank you for looking after him," his grandmother said.

"It's not a hard thing to do," I explained.

She cocked her head, sympathy showing in her eyes. "He's certainly charming…easy to love someone like that."

I nodded, knowing it would *definitely* be easy to love someone like him. "Nice meeting you," I said before turning away from her and walking to my car parked on the grass on the other side of the bridge.

I slipped inside my car and texted Izzy. **An interesting thing happened last night…**

Izzy: You hooked up with a hot guy?

Me: You're warm.
Izzy: Hot girl?
I laughed. **Cold.**
Izzy: I'm working. Just tell me.
Me: A spirit.

My phone rang immediately. Izzy's name was on the screen. I lifted it to my ear but she was talking before I could even say hello.

"Girl, what the hell is going on over there?"

"I know it's crazy."

"I can think of a lot of words for it," she said.

"It doesn't even matter," I sighed. "I think he was just making a point."

"What kind of point elicits a kiss?" she asked.

"I told him about being a virgin and Rick cheating. He told me I was missing out and then kissed me."

She grew silent.

I instantly regretted telling her. I should have just kept it my embarrassing secret.

"How was it?" she finally asked.

"The kiss?"

"Yes, the freaking kiss!"

"Amazing," I said, not even trying to hide my gushing. "But he hasn't said a word about it since it happened, so…"

Her voice grew serious. "Nora?"

I closed my eyes, knowing a lecture was coming.

"He knows how this ends," she said. "And, he doesn't want to break your heart."

"But what if he wakes up?"

"Do you think he's gonna wake up?" she asked.

"Truthfully?" I thought about him in that bed. The tubes. The machines. "It doesn't look good."

"So, I think you already know that whatever's going on is short-lived."

"Yeah," I agreed.

She grew silent again.

Why'd I text her? Did I want her to make me feel worse than I already did? Did I want her to be the voice of reason? Or, did I just need someone else to know so that I knew I wasn't crazy?

"You know," she finally, "who said you can't have some fun with him while he's still here?"

I hadn't expected her to say that. "But I told you, he was either making a point or regrets doing it in the first place since he's acting like it didn't happen."

"You know how guys are," she said. "Spirits are no different."

I laughed. "Get back to work."

"Love you, girl."

"I know. Right back at ya."

After hanging up the phone, I thought about the kiss and Izzy's take on it. I knew nothing could come from it given the fact that I was human and he was…well not exactly human. But, I also knew how good the kiss made me feel. And how good it felt to be around him. If I went into this knowing it was temporary, knowing I'd rather feel good for a short time than never feel this way at all, what could go wrong?

I eventually opened my car door and stepped out, climbing slowly down the hill to where I could see that Kyler lay back on the grass with his eyes closed by the edge of the river.

"How are you doing?" I asked as I sat down beside him.

He sat up, dragging his fingers through his hair. "I can't remember anything. I have no recollection of that night. Like nothing."

"Maybe I can ask Melanie more questions." I bumped him with my shoulder. "You know how much she likes me."

"That might not be a terrible idea."

"No?" I asked, surprised he thought so.

"Maybe you can tell her you can see me."

I scoffed. "Not sure she wants to hear that. She's already possessive of you."

"I can't even remember dating her."

"Well, she seemed to think you guys were supposed to get married someday."

His eyes grew wide. "She said that?"

"She didn't have to. I could tell by the daggers she was shooting at me."

He rolled his eyes. "Girls."

I rolled mine. "Spirits."

He smirked before staring back out at the river. The sun had begun to set in the distance casting an orange glow upon the early evening.

"I could visit some of your friends," I began. "They would've been at the party too, right?"

"Yeah."

"Maybe they can shed some light on your state of mind at the party when you left."

He looked over at me. "You'd do that?"

"Of course."

"Why do you keep helping me?"

"Because you keep haunting me," I teased.

He reached over and placed his hand on mine. Goosebumps erupted on my skin. What I wouldn't give for him to lean over and kiss me again. To let me know I hadn't imagined the feelings growing between us. "I really appreciate you," he said.

It was as if all the air had been sucked from my lungs.

He was friend-zoning me.

He was making it clear it had been a mistake to kiss me.

But, after all I'd been through with Rick and Zoe, I could do it too. I could wear a brave face and play it off as something insignificant too. "Stop trying to butter me up. I'm already helping you. It's not like I have big plans tonight anyway."

He forced a smile, though I could tell his mind was on the accident and his inability to remember it.

"Where do you wanna go?"

"My boy Bono works about a mile away at The Taco Shop."

"You sure he still works there?"

"Yeah, I've been haunting his ass too." He bumped me with his shoulder. "He's an open book. He'll tell you whatever you wanna know."

"Let's go see Bono," I said, pushing myself to my feet. Kyler followed me back to my car and we took off for The Taco Shop. "Your gram was lovely," I said. "She really loved you."

A whoosh of air passed through his lips. "And now, she's just a memory."

"Isn't that what we all become?" I asked, my eyes jumping between him and the road. "People will think of us sometimes or tell stories about us once in a while, but ultimately we're nothing more than memories when we go."

"Sad, isn't it?"

"Extremely," I agreed.

"But that's why *you* have to live life to the fullest while you still can."

"What are you trying to say?" I asked.

"*You* need to make memories. Create the stories people will tell about you when you're gone," he said.

"I do that," I argued.

He cocked his head. "Other than work, you haven't had a single plan since I met you."

"I've been busy with you."

He scoffed. "Don't miss out on things because you're afraid of getting hurt. You'll regret it."

"Look at you all motivating and stuff."

He shrugged. "What can I say? I'm amazing."

I laughed as I pulled into the parking lot of The Taco Shop, parking by the pole that held the huge taco-shaped sign. I cut the engine and looked to Kyler who stared out the window at the run-down building.

"That's his car over there," he said.

"Great. You ready?"

He looked back at me. "Are you?"

"I'm a medium. I'm ready for anything."

He laughed as I opened my car door and stepped out. He met me in the front of the car and we walked toward the restaurant. A girl walked out and held the door for me as we stepped inside. There were no booths, just a counter with a big menu filling the length of the wall.

"That's him," Kyler said, pointing to a guy grilling up some meat on the large grill behind the counter.

"Can I help you?" another guy asked.

I looked around realizing I was the only one in line. "Oh, I was hoping to speak to Bono for a second."

Bono looked over his shoulder causing his shaggy blonde hair to fall in his eyes. Unfamiliarity flashed across his face, but then he smiled. "Hey, little lady? Have we met before?"

"No, I'm a friend of Kyler's."

The mention of Kyler's name caused Bono's slender face to fall. He dropped his spatula to the side of the grill and said something to the other guy, before removing his apron and walking around the counter to meet me. "What'd you say your name was?"

"Nora. I went to school with Kyler in Florida."

He nodded, his face still filled with sadness. "He was my bro."

"Still am, man," Kyler said, trying to comfort his friend.

Bono led me outside to a picnic table on the side of the building.

"He's still alive," I said as Bono sat down on top of the table.

"Have you seen him?" he asked.

I nodded as I sat in one of the only spots that didn't seem to have salsa dripped on it.

"Then you know it's fucking terrible seeing him like that."

I thought back to the sight of him in that bed with the tubes and machines. "Do you still visit him?"

"I can't anymore. He wasn't waking up and every time I went, I just left feeling guilty."

"Why does he feel guilty?" Kyler asked.

"Guilty?" I asked.

"I shouldn't have let him leave the party."

"Was he drunk?"

"Nah. But that bitch Melanie was ragging on him and he'd had enough."

"What?" Kyler asked.

"Enough of what?" I asked.

"He was gonna dump her ass. I told him to just do it at the party, but he wanted to sit her down where it was quiet and not at a wild party. He said he owed her that."

"Jesus Christ," Kyler said.

"What?" I asked Kyler.

"He was gonna dump her," Bono repeated, thinking I'd asked him the question.

"I kind of remember that," Kyler said, excitement in his voice. "It's faint, but I remember."

"Did she know he was gonna break up with her?" I asked Bono.

"Everyone knew," Bono said.

"Why?" I asked.

"You've gotta know Melanie. She's kinda crazy."

"Yeah, we've met."

"She'd been crushing on Ky since high school. They only started dating the summer before the accident. He was lonely and she was always throwing herself at him."

"She *was* always throwing herself at me," Kyler said as if it was slowly coming back to him.

"So, he gave in?" I asked.

"Pretty much. I thought he was gonna kick her to the curb before going back to school, but she wasn't hearing it. She said they'd make the long-distance thing work."

"She wouldn't let me break up with her," Kyler said, recollection flashing in his eyes as he began pacing around the picnic table. "She said I could see other people while I was away, but we'd meet up when I was home. I agreed, thinking I could avoid her when I got home. But then she showed up at the party acting like we were still together. I couldn't take it."

"So, what do you think happened on the bridge?" I asked, directing the question at both of them.

"Icy roads," Bono answered.

Kyler tunneled his hands through his hair with pain etched into every line on his face.

"Worst night of my fucking life," Bono said, his eyes avoiding mine.

"I know it's hard to see him…the way he is now," I said to Bono. "But I think it helps when he has visitors."

"Yeah. Maybe I'll stop by," he said, though his words didn't hold much conviction.

"Can I ask you something else?"

He met my eyes. "Shoot."

"What's your favorite memory of Kyler?"

Amusement fluttered across his face.

"What?" I asked, eager to know what brought about the reaction.

"He was such an idiot sometimes," he said, laughing at his own words.

Kyler stopped pacing and looked to his friend. "Woah, Dude. Don't."

"A couple of us convinced him we were gonna streak across the football field on senior day," Bono said through his laughter.

"Asshole," Kyler cursed, though amusement twitched the corners of his lips.

Bono couldn't catch his breath he was laughing so hard. "He showed up naked and all of us were pissing our pants because we were all wearing clothes with no intention of streaking."

"Oh my God," I said, as visions of him naked in front of everyone flashed in my mind.

Kyler's cheeks were flushed but he was laughing.

"It was the funniest thing I've ever seen," Bono said.

"What happened?" I asked.

"He said, 'fuck it' and ran out there anyway. Everyone thought it was awesome."

I looked to Kyler with raised brows.

"The girls loved it," he assured me.

"He had this way of turning bad situations good," Bono added. "You know what I mean?"

I nodded, knowing Kyler did have a way of lighting up a room. "If you could say one more thing to him," I said to Bono, "what would you say?"

Bono pondered the thought for a minute. "I'd tell him I love him. And miss him. Things just aren't the same without him."

I glanced to Kyler whose eyes had blurred with tears.

"I'm sure he feels the same way," I assured Bono.

He ticked his head toward the shop. "I should probably head back inside."

I nodded. "Thanks for talking to me. I know you were a great friend to him."

Bono shot me a sad smile before hopping off the picnic table and taking off toward the shop.

I turned to Kyler, but he'd already taken off for the car. I was left sitting alone on a dirty taco shop picnic table feeling exhausted by all that Bono—and Kyler— had revealed.

I gave him the time he clearly needed, then headed back to my car and slipped into the driver's seat.

"Thanks," Kyler said without looking at me.

"You don't have to thank me, streaker."

He chuckled. "You liked that, didn't you?"

"Loved it," I assured him before starting the engine and pulling out onto the road.

Darkness had fallen and an uncomfortable silence descended upon the car. I could tell Kyler was mulling over everything that Bono had said and he'd remembered. I couldn't blame him. It had been a lot for one day. I just wished I knew what he needed from me in that moment. Maybe he wanted my silence. Unfortunately, for him, I hated awkward silences.

"So, you remember Melanie now?" I finally said.

"Yeah."

"How's that make you feel?"

He shrugged.

"Did it help you remember anything about the accident?"

He shook his head. "No, and it's driving me crazy."

"I seem to remember a wise person once telling me not to beat myself up over stuff I can't control."

I'd hoped that would make him smile, but it didn't.

"You remembered a lot all at once," I assured him. "It'll come back to you with time."

He grunted, telling me he wasn't so sure—and he didn't feel like talking.

Once we returned to my house, he went directly to the sofa and lay down, placing a throw pillow over his eyes. I knew he didn't need to sleep, since he couldn't actually do it, but he wanted to be left alone.

Taking the hint, I rummaged through the kitchen, grabbed a box of crackers and some cheese slices, and tiptoed upstairs. Hopefully, he'd be back to normal in the morning and want to talk about it.

CHAPTER 10

When I left for the café the next morning, Kyler wasn't on my sofa. I knew everything that had happened yesterday had been a lot for him. And, while I wanted him to have the space he needed, I also selfishly worried that he'd never return. Had I pushed him away? Had I enabled him to travel wherever he needed to go now? Had I been the catalyst for him crossing over?

Emptiness crept into my chest—then my heart.

Never before had I allowed a spirit to become such a big part of my life. And this was exactly the reason why. I shouldn't be left feeling guilty or empty or sad.

My shift was a long one, given Christmas was less than a week away and shoppers were out in full force. Daci asked me to stay longer and since I could use the money, I stayed until six. I grabbed my coat from the back room before stepping into the parking lot.

"Hey."

Kyler was leaning against the wall to my right. Relief washed over me knowing he hadn't disappeared. "Hey."

"Can I walk you home?"

I looked around the vacant parking lot. "I don't see a better offer."

He smiled but I could see the sadness behind it. We walked in silence through the alley between the buildings and then out onto the crowded sidewalk. I wondered where he'd been. I wondered what he'd been thinking about. But, I would not be the first one to speak. If I'd pushed him yesterday, I would not do the same thing tonight.

We eventually turned onto my street. Partygoers filled the lawn of one of the party houses. Every light in the house was on and people filled the first-floor rooms. The bass from the loud music inside rattled the road.

"Looks like a fun party," Kyler noted.

"End of semester rager," I said.

"You really never go out?" he asked, a touch of sympathy in his voice.

"Only when forced."

He chuckled, though it was short-lived once he looked ahead at my house. "Looks like you've got company."

There was a red sports car parked in the driveway. "Shit."

His eyes cut to mine. "Who is it?"

My insides crawled at the sight of Rick sitting on my front steps, his elbows resting on his knees and his hands folded in front of him. He lifted his head and smiled as I moved to the walkway.

"Him," I muttered.

"Tell him to fuck off," Kyler said.

I was in no mood to deal with Rick. Just like with Zoe, I'd somehow managed to avoid him since the beach. He stood up, burying his hands in his coat pockets and waiting for me to get closer. A mixture of hate, annoyance, and disgust flooded my body all at once.

"You okay?" Kyler asked.

"Perfect," I grumbled before I moved to the steps that Rick blocked. "What are you doing here?"

"I wanted to see you," he said as if a single day hadn't passed since I found him cheating on me.

"I've got nothing to say to you." I moved around him and up the steps to the door.

His footsteps sounded behind me. "I'm sorry, Nora. I never meant to hurt you."

"I'm not hurt," I assured him as I slipped the key into the lock.

"I meant when it happened—the way it happened," he explained.

"Oh, you mean at the beach? Thanks for ruining my favorite place for me. Totally appreciate your kindness. But rest assured. I'm over it," I said as I unlocked the door. "You and me, that is. Not the ruining the beach thing. *That* really sucks."

"Well, I'm not over it," he said. "You were the best thing that ever happened to me."

"Oh my God. This dude is so lame," Kyler said, already standing inside my living room as I pushed the door open and stepped inside.

I turned to face Rick who tried to step inside. I threw out my palm and pressed it to his chest. "Have you said everything you wanted to say?" I asked as his eyes dropped to my hand on him.

"Nora?" he pled, realizing I wasn't letting him inside my house.

"I hope you feel better now that you got that off your chest because, let's be honest, that's what this was all about, right? You clearing your conscience now that the two of you broke up?"

His eyes cast down.

"Goodbye, Rick. Don't ever come back here." I dropped my hand from his chest and slammed the door in his face. *Damn, that felt good.*

"Badass," Kyler said from somewhere in my living room.

I chuckled as I turned to face him.

"He's such a tool," he said.

"He is, isn't he?" I studied Kyler just a few feet away from me. Rick was nothing compared to him. He was untrustworthy while Kyler was honest. He was plain while Kyler's good looks could stop traffic. He was dull while Kyler's personality could fill a room. He was a terrible kisser while Kyler was perfection.

There was a knock on the front door.

"Want me to kick his ass?" Kyler asked.

I shook my head, knowing I could handle Rick. He was nothing to me. *He* was just a memory. Since I hadn't moved away from the door, I flung it back open. Izzy pushed her way inside pulling two suitcases behind her.

"Iz!" I screeched.

"Surprise!" she sang, dropping her suitcases and hugging me as we both jumped around.

We finally released each other. "I thought you were working?" I said.

"Total lie to throw you off," she said, proud of herself for keeping her return a secret. "Was I interrupting anything?" Her eyes moved around the living room, sweeping right over Kyler who had dropped down onto the sofa.

"Kyler's on the sofa," I explained.

"Oh really?" Izzy asked with insinuation in her tone.

"You told her about me?" he asked with raised brows.

"Well, you're the third roommate now, aren't you?" I said.

"What's he saying?" Izzy asked.

"He just asked if I'd told you about him."

"Has she ever," Izzy said, leaving it at that—though *that* was enough to let on that I'd been talking to her about him.

"Rick just left," I said.

Anger filled her features. "Why was that douchebag here?"

"Because he realizes he fucked up," Kyler said.

"Because he and Zoe broke up."

"Figures," Izzy said.

"And he wanted to clear his conscience," I explained.

"Tell me you punched him again," she said.

"No. I've matured a lot since the summer and held back my anger this time. Now tell me, how long will you be home?"

"I leave the day after Christmas."

"That still gives us a week," I said.

"Go get dressed. I wanna go out," she said. "I need drinks and girl time," she explained.

"Why don't you hit up that party down the block," Kyler suggested.

"You're really pushing that party," I said to him.

"What party?" Izzy asked.

"Didn't you see the one on the corner?"

"At Tim and Al's?" she asked.

"That's the one."

A big smile spread across her face.

"What's that look?" I asked.

"I've been working twelve-hour shifts for three months straight. I feel like I've aged ten years in those three months. I need to feel like a twenty-two-year-old again," she said.

I looked from Kyler to Izzy, unsure if a party was what I needed. But I missed my friend desperately. And, a girl's night sounded like a good idea. "Fine."

Izzy screamed. "Let me go shower. Make yourself look hot. We're finding ourselves some guys tonight." With that, she winked at me so Kyler couldn't see then pulled her suitcases up the stairs and disappeared upstairs.

"Gonna make yourself look hot?" Kyler asked me.

I spun to look at him, hating that he still hadn't mentioned our kiss. He didn't have the right to now act all cheeky about me looking hot for a guy. "You heard Izzy. I've gotta find myself a guy tonight." I broke his stare and hurried upstairs, knowing I deserved this night. And, I deserved someone who wouldn't act like they hadn't kissed me when they most certainly had.

CHAPTER 11

I slipped on my tightest jeans and a sparkly green off-the-shoulder top. My hair hung in loose waves, my eyes were smoky, and my lipstick made my normal lips pouty and shiny. I met Izzy downstairs and she released a long, drawn-out whistle as I stepped into the living room. "Someone looks ready to find a man," she said, her own outfit looking similar to mine.

I laughed before glancing to Kyler still on the sofa. He shot me a sad smile. "You look really pretty."

I wished the hot guy Izzy wanted me to find tonight wasn't already sitting in my living room. "Thanks."

"Have fun tonight," he said.

"We will," I said as I followed Izzy out the front door.

"Don't wait up," she called back toward the house.

I looked at her, confused.

"What?" she asked. "He's here, right?"

"Yeah," I said as we stepped outside and made our way to the sidewalk.

"No reason we can't make him a little jealous," she said as our wedges carried us toward the music pouring out of the house on the corner.

"Why would he be jealous?" I asked.

"Because you look hot."

I glanced down at myself and wondered if that's what he saw when he looked at me.

"And, because something's going on with you and the spirit—"

"Stop. It sounds ridiculous hearing you say it out loud," I said. "Nothing's going on with us."

She scoffed as we walked up the path to the house. People we knew from school waved or called out to us as we made our way inside and to the bar in the kitchen.

"Izzy!" Al, one of the guys who lived there, called as he grabbed her in a bear hug and lifted her off her feet.

She threw back her head and laughed, definitely missing her carefree college days.

"Hey, Nora," he said once he set her back down. "Where's Red?"

"We don't run in the same circles anymore," Izzy explained, saving me the explanation.

"That's a shame. She's hot," he said.

My stomach churned. People didn't know the real Zoe. Hell, I didn't know the real Zoe.

I watched Al pour multiple liquors into our red cups and very little of anything else.

"Drinks for my neighbors," he said as he turned and handed them to us.

I sipped my drink, wincing as the burn traveled down my throat. "I guess it's gonna be that kind of night."

"The best kind!" Izzy declared with her cup raised.

We spent the next couple of hours dancing in the cleared-out living room with guys we didn't know and who were probably too young for us.

"What's your name, beautiful?" a guy whispered in my ear from behind, his hands guiding my hips.

"You already know. It's Beautiful," I lied.

"No shit?"

"No shit. My mom was eccentric," I said.

I watched as Izzy had her own freshman grinding up on her. I laughed, loving the attention but knowing full well we'd be going home alone.

"Nora!" Hannah, a girl I knew from my dorm sophomore year, danced over to me. "Where've you been, girl?"

"Working at the café," I explained.

"You need to come out with us to the clubs," she said. "Being legal rocks."

"I'll go," my dance partner offered.

"There's no way you're even twenty-one," I said.

"I will be…in three years."

Hannah and I burst into laughter. "Have you met…" I glanced over my shoulder at him. "What was your name?"

"Derrick," he said with a grin.

I looked back to Hannah. "Have you met my very young friend Derrick?"

"Haven't had the pleasure," she said as the song ended and another began.

"I think the lady wants a dance," I said to him.

"Thanks, Beautiful," he said as he finally released my hips and moved his hands to Hannah's.

"You're welcome," I teased Hannah before weaving my way through the dance floor. I found Al at the bar in the kitchen and he mixed me up another concoction which burned just as much as the others going down. But I didn't care. I needed this night. I needed my friend back. I need to forget Rick and Zoe.

"You ready to head home?" Izzy asked sometime after one.

"Home?" I asked, my words slurred. "They were just starting to play good music."

She laughed. "Come on. I'm exhausted."

"Fine," I relented, downing the rest of my drink.

Outside, the cold rush of air sent goosebumps popping up all over my skin. Totally rethinking the no jacket *and* amount I'd drank because each step brought me sideways. Izzy wrapped her arm around me and we weaved our way toward home.

"I think we drank too much," she slurred.

"Me too," I slurred back.

We burst into laughter.

"I needed this," she said.

"Me too."

"You don't need me to go out and have fun, you know," Izzy said.

"I know, it's just not the same without you here."

"Don't guilt-trip me. I already miss it," she said.

"Oh my God, I'm not trying to. I just mean…going out isn't fun without you."

"I told you, you need a man."

"My vibrator works just fine," I assured her.

Our laughter cut through the cold night air as we stumbled our way up the front steps. I struggled with my key, somehow unlocking the door as Izzy pushed it open. We fell inside, landing unceremoniously on the floor. We howled in laughter, tears rolling down our cheeks.

"Looks like you girls had fun," Kyler said.

My laughter ceased, forgetting he'd be wide awake when we got home.

"What's wrong?" Izzy asked.

"Our roommate doesn't sleep," I explained.

Her head whipped around as she pushed herself to a sitting position. "Where is he?"

"On the sofa," I explained.

He stared at me on the floor beside her. "I expected you two to bring those hot guys home with you."

"Then why are you sitting here cramping our style?" I slurred.

He bit back a smile. "Did someone have a lot to drink tonight?"

"Someone did," I said, almost wanting to stick it to him for disregarding our kiss.

"Friend here not hearing both sides of the conversation," Izzy interjected as she pushed herself unsteadily to her feet.

"Sorry." I stood up unsteadily but willed myself not to fall in front of Kyler—again.

"I need to sleep. Or puke," she said as she headed to the stairs.

"Do you need my help?" I asked.

She swatted her hand in my direction as she disappeared upstairs.

"How was the party?" Kyler asked once we were alone.

I couldn't bring myself to turn around. I was drunk and he was gorgeous and maddening and a spirit.

"Hook up with any guys?" he kept at it.

I spun around. "Why did you kiss me?"

His head hitched back. "What?"

"You're always honest with me," I said, hating that I was slurring. "Why did you kiss me?"

His eyes locked on mine and though it looked like he might answer me, he didn't.

"Do you pity me?"

His brows furrowed. "Pity you?"

"Because…you know…"

"Nora, I don't pity you."

"Why do I feel like that's the first lie you've told me?"

He was inches from my face before I knew how he'd even gotten there. His hands cupped my cheeks, his eyes peering into mine. "I've never lied to you."

"Why'd you kiss me?" I asked again.

The seconds ticked by as his eyes riveted between mine. "Because I couldn't imagine never kissing you."

I swallowed down the lump of emotion in my throat.

"I am very aware that I could disappear without warning," he continued, his eyes now focused on my mouth. "But, I'm also aware that you're beautiful and smart and funny and someone I can't seem to be without."

Tears stung my eyes.

His eyes lifted to mine. "*That's* why I kissed you."

I lunged forward, my lips crashing into his. He staggered back a few steps, clearly unprepared for my drunken attack. But he seemed to be on board as his arms slipped around to my back and lips moved in tandem with mine. I draped my arms over his shoulders and walked him backward until the backs of his knees hit the sofa. I urged him down, climbing on his lap and straddling him as I kept the lead, my lips devouring his. His hands settled on my ass as our tongues dueled for control, tangling in delicious sync. My hips found a rhythm. I couldn't stop myself from grinding against him. And, despite everything I knew to be reality, his erection pressed between my thighs sending zingers through me like someone who was very much there and alive.

I was desperate for a breath, but he pulled away first. Our chests heaved as we stared at each other, our eyes heavy with need. A slow smirk slipped across his lips. "What are the odds you'll remember any of this in the morning?"

"Fifty-fifty," I said.

He chuckled, leaning in and kissing me soft and slow before pulling back. "Come on. Let me walk you to your room."

An embarrassed flush spread over my body. Was he rejecting me? *Had* he been pitying me? "I can find it myself," I grumbled, feeling like a little kid being ordered to their room. I attempted to crawl off his lap, but he held me there.

"That's too bad. I was hoping you were gonna let me sleep in your bed with you tonight."

"Why? Is the sofa uncomfortable?" I asked.

He cocked his head. "No. But I bet you're a good snuggler."

"Probably not."

He huffed his frustration. "Jesus Christ, Nora. I want to hold you. Can't I just do that?"

I tried to ignore the tsunami rolling through my stomach. "You sure I'll be able to resist you?" I asked, referencing the conversation that led to our first kiss.

He chuckled. "Oh, you definitely won't be able to resist me. Luckily, I'm a gentleman who'd never pressure you to do something you weren't ready to do."

"Who said I'm not ready?" As soon as the words left my mouth, I gasped, shocked that I said them out loud.

"You're drunk," he said. "And while it's one of the most adorable things I've seen in a long time, I'm not about to take advantage of that."

"So, if I start stripping, you'd stop me?"

He laughed. "No. But, I wouldn't let it go any further."

I rolled my eyes. "Says the streaker."

He suppressed a smile. "You'll appreciate this in the morning. I promise."

Embarrassed—and rejected, I attempted to crawl off his lap again.

His hands seized my arms and he pulled me back toward him, his lips capturing mine for a long glorious kiss. He was assuring me that he wasn't rejecting me forever. He was just halting the brakes tonight when the chances were high that I wouldn't remember it in the morning. His lips abandoned mine and moved to my ear. "Let's go upstairs." He urged me off his lap.

Once we both stood, he linked his fingers with mine and led me up the stairs—likely making sure I didn't end up on my ass again. Regardless, the gesture had my heartbeat skyrocketing. How was this even happening? If I was dreaming—if this wasn't even remotely possible—I didn't want to know.

There were four rooms on the second floor. We passed the open bathroom, then Izzy's closed door, and the spare room that was supposed to be Zoe's. At the end of the hallway, we walked into my room. Kyler took in the crystal chandelier in the center of my ceiling, the heap of pillows on my bed, and all the hand-painted art on my walls. "Did you paint these?" he asked, taking in all the coastal scenery boasting vivid blues, yellows, and pinks—my favorite colors to work with.

"Yeah. I started after my dad passed away to keep my mind busy. It just kinda stuck."

"Well, for what it's worth, I think you're incredibly talented."

I wished him in my bedroom complementing my art didn't feel so normal.

His eyes moved to the nightstand that held a small light and framed photo of my parents and me when I was five outside of Disney World. He looked back to me. "You look like your mom."

"Yeah. We both have the same freckles on our noses."

He examined my freckles for a beat before he glanced back at the photo. "Your dad was healthy in this picture?"

I nodded.

His eyes made one more sweep of my room before he looked back at me. "I like your room."

"Haven't you been up here?" I asked.

"I wouldn't invade your privacy like that."

"Not my privacy, just my life?" I sassed.

He moved in front of me, placing his lips to my ear. "I don't see you complaining."

Tremors rocked through me and my body hummed like a damn live wire.

He chuckled against my ear. "Get your pajamas on." He slipped off his sneakers and moved to my bed, pushing my throw pillows to the floor and climbing under my comforter. He dropped his arms over his eyes. "Go ahead. I'm not looking."

I grabbed my skimpiest pajamas—booty shorts and a tank top—from my drawer and changed into them in the bathroom then brushed my teeth. When I returned to my room, Kyler was on his side with his cheek resting in his palm. "Didn't trust me not to peek?" he asked as his eyes raked over my body.

I placed my clothes in my laundry basket. Knowing he was watching my every move, I swayed my ass a little more than probably necessary as I moved over to my bed and climbed under the comforter. Kyler rolled me onto my side so I faced him and wrapped his arms around me. "Now this is so much better than the sofa."

My cheek was pressed into his chest as I relaxed in his arms. That's when the room began to spin, and I needed to close my eyes so I wouldn't vomit. He'd been right. If things did move any faster, I may not have remembered any of it. With my ear to his chest, I listened for a heartbeat. And, despite my need to hear one, the only one I heard was my own.

"You're a good snuggler," Kyler said, tightening his arms around me in a way that made me feel incredibly safe.

"No one's ever told me that," I said.

"That's a shame. You deserve so much more than you've been given."

"Stop bullshitting me."

"I'm not. You got stuck with a tool for an ex and an untrustworthy friend. You have spirits barging into your life expecting things from you but you gain nothing from helping them."

"Not true. I gained you."

He tightened his arms again and pressed his lips to the top of my head. "I'd give you the world if I could."

I said nothing, knowing he couldn't promise me anything. And I'd be a fool to expect him to. I just knew that everything felt right in his arms, and I'd take it for as long as I could get it. If that made me pathetic, then I was pathetic. But I was also happy.

"Good night, Nora."

"Good night, Kyler."

"Sweet dreams," he said.

"They will be," I said, and those were the last words I remember before sleep pulled my drunken self under.

CHAPTER 12

My phone alarm beeped in some far-off place. I knew it was beeping, but I couldn't pull myself from the darkness to shut it off.

"Nora?" Kyler whispered.

My head whipped up from his chest, pounding like a son-of-a-bitch. His arms were wrapped around me stopping me from jumping away completely.

"Uh, oh. Did you forget I was here?" he asked.

"I…" I struggled to recall last night. The party. The drinks. Kissing Kyler.

"Is it coming back to you yet?" he asked.

"A little. Did we?"

"Kiss? Yes."

My heart rate spiked. That wasn't exactly what I'd been thinking. "I remember that."

"Liar."

"No, I do. I just don't remember what happened after that." I cringed, hating that I needed to ask the next question. "How did we get up here?"

"I asked if I could sleep with you."

My body tensed. I didn't remember any of that.

He chuckled. "Not like that. Just sleep. That's all we did."

"Why?" I asked.

"Because if we do anything more, I want you to remember."

I winced. "Was I that bad?"

"You were that funny. But I assure you, you were out within minutes of getting up here."

I nodded, vaguely recalling something like that.

"How are you feeling?"

"Like I drank too much."

He chuckled. "But you also had fun. You were laughing so hard when you got home. It looked good on you."

"I should get up," I said, pulling away from Kyler's arms. "I have a reading today, then a shift at the cafe."

"You wanna do something tonight?"

"Do something?" I asked.

"Yeah. I have a good idea for something we can do and you won't get any funny looks for talking to yourself."

"Okay."

"Okay," he agreed.

* * *

With my head still hurting from the night before, I rushed through the alley, cut into the back parking lot, then ducked through the back door of the café. I checked my phone as I shimmied off my coat and hung it on one of the wall hooks. I was definitely late.

I hurried out front. A girl with blonde hair was already seated with her back to me at my table. "Sorry I'm late,"

I said out of breath as I stepped up beside her with my hand extended. That's when a cold chill rushed up my spine.

"Hello again," Melanie said with a smug grin on her face.

I lowered my hand. "*You're* Lanie?" I looked around to see if I was being punked.

"It's what my family calls me," she said, knowing she'd pulled one over on me. "Sit down. I'm excited to begin."

"How did you know…?"

"You didn't actually think I was going to let you visit my boyfriend and not do my research." Her condescending look told me she knew I'd lied. Lied about going to school with Kyler. Lied about everything. "And your car had a Virginia license plate, so…"

"Why are you here?" I asked, skipping pretenses.

"Because I think you've seen Kyler and that's why you've been sniffing around."

How was I getting out of this one? "No…I…I heard what happened and I thought maybe I could help," I lied.

She tipped her head to the side, not buying my story. "So, you told Mrs. Fletcher why you were there?"

"Not exactly."

"How about Sue?"

"No," I admitted.

"Did you see anything while you were with him?" she asked, the tapping of her foot catching my attention. Was all her bravado an act? Was she nervous about something?

"No."

"Did you hear anything?"

I shook my head.

"I heard you went to see Bono."

My brows shot up. "Are you following me?"

She scoffed. "It's a small town. People talk. Why did you want to talk to him?"

"I knew they were friends."

Her brows inverted. "How would you know that?"

"I'm a medium. We tend to know stuff."

An old man materialized over Melanie's right shoulder. "She's a liar," he announced.

My eyes narrowed as I searched his weathered face for a clue of what he meant. "Did you lose a grandfather?" I asked.

Her head whipped around. "Why? Is he here?"

The old man held his index finger up to his lips.

"No. I was just wondering who you were hoping to communicate with on the other side," I lied. "You *are* here for a reading, right?"

"I want to communicate with my boyfriend, of course."

My stomach churned, the thought of him ever being with her was unfathomable. "He's still alive," I said. "I only hear from spirits who have crossed over."

"She doesn't want you to know," the old man said.

"Know what?" I asked.

"I didn't say anything," Melanie said.

"She doesn't want anyone to know," he said.

Melanie looked over her shoulder. "What are you looking at?" she snapped.

I shook my head. "I'm sorry. I'm just trying to focus."

"Are you trying to reach Kyler?"

"I can try," I lied. "Do you have anything with you that belonged to him?"

She reached into her handbag at her side and pulled out a folded red T-shirt.

"May I?"

She slowly handed it over to me. I placed my hand on it, as if testing it for a pulse, and closed my eyes. I knew he wouldn't materialize like other spirits did because he didn't seem to work like that. He'd walk through the door.

"It still smells like him," Melanie said.

I lifted it to my nose and the faint scent of cologne still lingered on the material. "What cologne is that?"

"He only wore Polo," she said.

If she wasn't sitting there watching me, I would have smelled it for longer. I'd wondered what he smelled like. "Does this shirt mean anything?"

"I got pushed into a pool at a party and needed something to wear. He took off his shirt for me. I never gave it back."

I pushed aside my jealousy knowing that was the kind of guy he was.

"Is he here?" she asked.

I looked around the area just to be sure, but he hadn't appeared. "I told you. I'm not sure this can work since he's still alive."

"Not really."

The way she said it turned my stomach. "Have you tried talking to him?" I asked.

"What's the point?"

I tried to hide my disgust. "The point is he may be able to hear you."

"Well, he doesn't speak, so I'll never know."

"They say regaling stories and familiar voices can speed up recovery in comatose patients."

"So, now you're a doctor?" she said.

"All I'm saying is maybe a medium isn't what you need."

She snatched his shirt from my hand. "I knew you'd be a scammer." She jumped to her feet and stormed out.

"Wow," Daci said, poking her head through the curtains. "I've seen them leave crying their eyes out. But never storming out."

I laughed. "You don't know the half."

She walked into my area and sat in the chair Melanie just vacated. "Try me."

"Her boyfriend is in a coma," I explained.

Her brows furrowed. "If he's not dead, what did she expect from you?"

I leaned in, lowering my voice in case Melanie returned. "I've seen him."

"Is that a first for you?" Daci asked.

I nodded. "I thought he was dead when he first showed up. *He* didn't even know he was still alive."

"So, he's stuck in limbo?" she asked.

"He has unfinished business. And, he doesn't want to cross over."

"Why do I get the feeling you didn't tell her you've seen him?" she asked.

I pursed my lips, unsure how much I should say.

"Is he hot?" she asked.

Nervous laughter escaped me. "What?"

"I'm getting hot guy vibes."

I buried my face in my hands.

"Oh. My. God," she said. "You need to tell me every juicy bit."

I dropped my hands. "He's very good looking."

"I knew it!"

"*Shhhh.*" My head whipped around, making sure Julie out front didn't hear us talking.

"Are you helping him figure out why he's still here?"

"I'm trying."

"Do you think he's gonna wake up?"

I sighed. "Question of the century."

"Why haven't you told me any of this?" she asked.

"It's complicated. I don't really get what's happening myself."

"What does that mean?"

"He's different than the others," I explained. "I can actually touch him."

"Shut the front door! You've touched him?" She was nearly jumping out of her seat.

I nodded.

"No way."

"Way."

"Jesus Christ," she said.

"Please don't tell anyone any of this."

She made the sign of a cross over her heart. "Cross my heart and—"

"Don't say it," I said.

She cocked her head. "And hope he lives."

Oh. I liked that one.

* * *

After my shift, I stopped by one of the boutiques on my way home. This one carried women's and men's clothes. I went to the back of the store where the accessories and fragrances lined the wall. I scanned through the bottles until I came upon the green bottle I'd been hoping to find. I picked it up and twisted off the cap. I closed my eyes and sniffed the nozzle, envisioning it on Kyler.

"Can I help you?" a woman asked.

My eyes popped open. "I'd like to purchase this please."

She took it from me and rang me out. I walked home with the bag in my hand excited I'd be able to have a small piece of him.

He wasn't on the sofa when I got home. But a glass of water and two Advil were on the table with a note from Izzy. She'd be staying at her parents' house tonight.

I showered then pulled on jeans and a pink cashmere sweater, knowing wherever he planned to take me, the outfit would work for the evening. It wasn't like he could take me anywhere that cost money. I guess there weren't many options for a night out with a spirit.

I dried and curled my hair before swiping on some light makeup and heading downstairs.

Kyler sat on the sofa and his eyes drifted over my outfit. "Hi there."

"Did you just get here?"

"A few minutes ago. Did you have a nice day?" he asked.

"Funny you should ask." I sat down beside him holding the bottle of cologne.

"What's this?"

"I heard it's what you wear."

"From who?"

"One guess."

Anger flashed in his eyes. "Where?"

"She was my reading."

"Why didn't you tell me?"

"I didn't know. And, it's not like I could've just called you on your phone."

"What'd she want?"

"Well, for one, to let me know she knew I lied about knowing you from school. And two, to speak to you on the other side."

He dropped his head back and groaned. "Did I speak to her?"

I laughed. "No. But, her grandfather showed up."

"What'd he have to say?" he asked.

"That she's keeping a secret."

His head shot upright. "What kind of secret?"

I shrugged. "He disappeared when I asked."

His eyes searched the ceiling as if trying to decipher the grandfather's cryptic message. "We need to find out."

"I know. But I can't force spirits to tell me anything."

"Let's go back to my house tomorrow. If she's there, I'll appear and speak to her. I'll find out what she's hiding."

I'm glad he was so certain she'd be forthcoming because I wasn't sure she'd want anyone knowing a secret even her grandfather didn't see fit to tell me. And, though I always tried to be positive, I had a sinking feeling that I knew what that secret might be.

"So…" He ticked his chin toward my hand, snapping me out of my thoughts. "Why'd you get the cologne?"

"Because I wanted to be able to smell you."

He grinned. "And? How do I smell?"

"Just like I imagined," I admitted.

He wrapped his arm around my shoulders and pulled me into his side. I couldn't help but nestle into his body as if the spot was made for me. "Why does this have to suck so much?"

"What?"

"Being caught between life and death."

"You can always stop being caught and wake up," I said.

"I'd give anything to be alive," he said.

"What would you do first?"

He was silent for a long time. "Introduce you to my parents."

"Shut up," I whined, embarrassed I'd clearly forced him into saying that.

"I'm serious. I want to do the normal stuff I can't do right now. I want to talk to people. I want to hug the people I care about. Oh, and I want to eat *fooooooood*."

Even though he was making light of his situation, I still hurt for him.

"You ready?" he asked, his eyes cutting down to me.

I sat up causing him to do the same. "Ready."

* * *

"Pull over," Kyler said, pointing to the side of the road he'd directed me to in a nearby town.

I pulled to a stop in front of a beautiful colonial home on our right. Christmas lights covered every surface of the exterior. Blowup decorations and retro blow-molds of snowmen, Santa Claus, Christmas carolers, and reindeer lined the landscape. Glowing snowflakes hung from the branches of the massive trees on either side of their walkway.

"Shut off your lights," he urged and I did. "Now, tune the radio to 98.5. The lights will move to the music."

I turned on the channel, and "Santa Clause is Coming to Town" played. The hopping lights on glowing arches on the roof moved in time to the music. "It's so pretty."

He smiled, his eyes focusing on mine. "I can't take you on a real date," he said. "And I really wanted to."

"This is perfect," I assured him.

We sat outside the home admiring the lights and listening to Christmas music for a long time. As abnormal as this was, it was the most normal I'd ever felt with a guy—and the most comfortable.

"I wanted my parents to do this to our house when I was a kid," Kyler said.

"They didn't want to?"

"My mom didn't want to put a bunch of staples into the vinyl siding, and my dad worried about the roof leaking if we added all that stuff up there," he explained.

"Yeah, I can see them not wanting to damage their beautiful home."

"But you'd think they'd want to make me happy. Being their only kid and all."

"*Spoiled* only kid," I amended for him.

He smiled. "Did you ever get lonely being an only child?"

I shrugged. "I always had Izzy a few houses down, so I felt like she was my sister. But, I guess, when I lost my dad, I really wished I had one."

"Will you have more than one child someday?" he asked.

"I don't know. I turned out okay, so one would be good. But, then again, I guess two would be a blessing."

He nodded his understanding.

"How about you? Did you get lonely?"

"No. But *now* I wish I had a sibling so my parents weren't alone. Like, if things going any more south, they've still got a kid." He looked away and I could tell his words were choking him up.

"Well, I'll make you this promise. Your parents are stuck with me. So, they better hear me out tomorrow. Because if they don't, it's going to make showing up at their door a lot harder."

He smiled and I could tell I'd pulled him from his sadness.

I lifted my head toward the illuminated house. "Do you remember bringing Melanie on any dates like this?"

"I don't think it was that kind of relationship," he admitted sheepishly.

"Yeah, I got that feeling from Bono," I said. "Did you date many girls at school?"

"Not sure if date is what you'd call it," he again admitted uncomfortably.

Even though a knot twisted in my gut, I got it. "If girls were willing to accept less than, why should you turn them down?"

"Yeah, well, hearing you say it that way makes me sound like a douchebag."

I wasn't about to disagree. If the shoe fit…

"But, I assure you," he continued. "I never cheated on anyone."

I didn't respond knowing he'd said that for my benefit. Because despite him screwing different girls, he didn't screw around on any of them. He was a better guy than Rick.

Kyler reached over and brushed a piece of hair away from my face sending a shiver rippling in its wake. "You gonna let me sleep in your bed tonight?" he asked.

I suppressed the smile that itched to burst through. "Maybe."

"Maybe?"

I shrugged, playing coy.

He chuckled. "I wonder what I need to do to convince you."

"I wonder," I mused.

* * *

Kyler pinned me to my bedroom door pressing open-mouthed kisses from my ear to my collarbone. The warmth spreading through my body *was* otherworldly. Through his jeans, his erection pressed between my thighs as he ground his hips against me, causing flutters down to my toes. Why hadn't it felt like this with Rick? Why hadn't I been ready to go all in like I found myself wanting to do with Kyler? Was it because Kyler was safe? Was it because Kyler could disappear any day?

My hands moved between us to the button on his jeans.

His hand seized my hands. "*Nora.*"

"What?" I asked, breathless and turned on.

"What are you doing?" he asked.

"You know what I'm doing."

"Are you sure?"

I looked him straight in the eyes. "You could disappear tomorrow and we'd never have this chance."

His head tipped to the side, his eyes questioning my response.

My fingers struggled with the button of his jeans. "Do these even come off?" I'd never seen him in anything except his black hoodie and jeans.

"Let's find out," he said, the rasp in his voice causing my fingers to tremble as the button slipped through the slot.

I released a deep breath before pushing his jeans down his legs.

"I guess they do," he said as he shucked his sneakers and shoved his jeans down the rest of the way, leaving him in a pair of boxers. "What next?" he asked.

I reached for the hem of his hoodie and tugged it up and over his head. *Dammit.* He had a white T-shirt beneath it.

"Do you want to see what's underneath?" he asked with a devious glint in his eyes.

I said nothing, just tugged the T-shirt up and over his head. "Seriously?" I grumbled as I took in the view.

He laughed. "Better than you expected?"

I lifted my hands to his chest. His skin felt unexpectedly smooth beneath my palms. My fingertips drifted over his muscular shoulders, down the perfect indentation between his pecs, over his chiseled abs then back up again.

"This is all very one-sided," he observed since I was still fully clothed.

I lifted my arms above me, giving him the go-ahead. He grasped the hem of my sweater and peeled it over my head leaving me in my pink bra. His gaze drifted down and his fingertips grazed my hip, leaving a trail of goosebumps in their wake.

I didn't wait for him. I unbuttoned my jeans and pushed them down, kicking them off until I stood in only my matching pink thong and bra.

His eyes drifted down again, this time hunger flashed in them. He grabbed my ass and lifted me off my feet. I yelped as I wrapped my legs around his hips and hung onto his shoulders. He lowered me to the bed, covering me with his body. Our bodies pressed together ignited a fire beneath my skin. His lips crashed down on mine as his erection, much more prominent through the thin material of his boxers, pressed between my thighs. The vigor of his kiss told me we'd moved past just making out. His hand slipped down my side, his fingertips creating a trail of heat. He played with the scrap of material holding my thong to my hip before slipping his fingertips beneath it. I sucked in a sharp breath.

"I won't do anything you don't want me to do," he said against my lips.

"I know," I said.

With featherlight precision, his fingers slipped along the back of my thong and down between the crack of my ass. I held my breath, uncertain of his next move. "I've got you," he whispered, moving his finger lower and over the material between my legs.

I released my breath. I'd never been this turned on by another human being in my entire life. I shook off the notion. He wasn't human. Not really anyway. But the second his fingers drifted under the material between my legs, he felt more human than anyone I'd ever met before. His fingertips glided over my wet folds, back and forth. Each time he grazed my clit, small tremors erupted. My eyes squeezed shut as the back of my head pushed into the pillow. My breathing became labored; my sighs heavy.

"Did he ever do this to you?" he whispered against my lips.

"Yes."

"Did he ever use his mouth?"

"No," I breathed, knowing he was now realizing how PG-13 my relationship with Rick had really been.

"Did you want him to?" he asked.

"No."

"Do you want *me* to?" he asked his fingers plunging inside me.

"*God*," I groaned as my back arched off the bed. "*Yes.*"

A devious chuckle escaped him. "Tonight?"

"*Yes.*"

A low chuckle rumbled in his chest.

I gasped as his thumb pressed against my clit while his fingers curled inside me. I shifted my hips, lifting them as much as I could with the weight of him on top of me as his fingers pumped in and out.

"Does this feel good?"

"*Soooo good*," I moaned.

His fingers continued moving. A spiral of sensations began to coil inside me. Even though my eyes were closed, I squeezed them and focused on that tiny ball of sensation swirling inside me, building and building. I held my breath.

"Not yet, Nora," he taunted, removing his fingers with me right on the cusp.

"What…"

He moved down my body, pulling my panties down my legs.

I closed my eyes as his mouth replaced his fingers, his tongue moving against my clit.

"Je-sus," I breathed as the sensations began to swirl again, building and building as he licked his way around my clit, torturing it with exact precision as my body let go. The swirl of sensation released, tremors rocking through me as Kyler kept at it. Wave after wave. Shiver after shiver. Then, an invisible hum radiated over my body.

Kyler's tongue disappeared. He moved back up my body and pressed his lips to mine. "That's what it should feel like when you're with someone special."

I stared at him speechlessly—for so many reasons.

He shifted off me, rolling me onto my side away from him. He wrapped his arms around me and held me as my heavy breaths continued, the satisfied buzz still radiating from my skin.

"What about you?" I asked.

"What about me?"

"Isn't it your turn?"

"Is that what your ex made you think?" he asked.

I shrugged, though his strong arms around me made it near impossible.

"Well, that's not how it works. Tonight was about you. *Only* you."

"But won't you turn blue?"

He pulled me closer to him as his chest shook with laughter. "I'll be okay," he assured me. "Are *you* okay?"

"Very," I sighed.

He lowered his lips to my shoulder and peppered my skin with feather-light kisses. "Oh, sweet Nora. Why did I have to meet you now?"

"Because you needed me."

"I still need you," he said.

The most heartbreaking thing about it was, I felt the same way. I needed him in ways I had no right to. And, *that* scared the hell out of me.

CHAPTER 13

It was difficult to make eye contact with Kyler after last night. But I thought I played it off well by getting up, showering, and dressing while he still lay in my bed. I figured he was waiting for me to say something, but how did you verbalize how it felt to be with someone who made you feel special? Someone who put you first? Someone who was not really there?

I was seriously hopeless.

"So, we gonna talk about last night?" he finally said once we were in the car on the way to his parents' house.

"What would you like to talk about?" My eyes cut to his.

He cocked his head.

"Do you have specific questions?" I asked feeling more awkward than ever.

He stifled a smile, likely enjoying watching me squirm. "No, just an overall observation."

"It was nice," I said.

"Nice?" he asked.

"Very nice?" I asked, checking if that was what he wanted me to say.

"Very nice?" he asked, bemused.

"Look, you're not making this easy," I said.

"What?"

"Being in this small space with you after what we did," I snapped.

He stifled a smile. "And why's that?"

"Because it's making me uncomfortable."

"You never have to be uncomfortable with me," he said.

"You weren't Mr. Motormouth this morning either," I argued.

"I'm worried about today."

Now I felt ridiculous. I'd been making this about me when he was nervous about his own situation. "Why didn't you just tell me that? I thought you were regretting last night."

"Why would I regret last night?" he asked, confused.

I shrugged. "I don't know."

He rolled his eyes. "Girls."

I rolled mine. "Spirits."

He smiled and all was right in the world again. "So, what's the plan for today?"

"Tell your parents who I am and what I can do."

He nodded, but he didn't appear too confident that this would actually work.

We pulled up in front of his home a short time later. Sue's van and two dark sedans were in the driveway.

"Those are my parents' cars," he explained.

I parked in front of the house, killing the engine and staring at the house. "Please let this work," I said before pushing open my door and meeting Kyler on the sidewalk. Side by side, we made our way up the walkway.

"You got this, Nora. I believe in you."

"Yeah, let's hope your parents do too," I muttered as I climbed the steps and rang the doorbell. Like the last time, I could hear the loud chime echo inside.

The door opened and I sucked in a breath. Mrs. Fletcher stared at me as if she recognized me and wasn't happy I had the nerve to return. She attempted to close the door in my face when my hand shot out and I stopped it. "Please," I pled. "I need to speak to you about Kyler."

"Oh, hello," Sue said as she stepped up beside her. "She's a good girl," she informed Mrs. Fletcher. "She's visited before."

Mrs. Fletcher glanced over her shoulder at Sue. I hoped she didn't fire her for letting me in when she wasn't home.

"So nice to see you again," Sue said to me. "I'm sure Kyler would appreciate seeing you again."

Mrs. Fletcher turned back to me. "You were in my house?"

"I promise you. I came with nothing but good intentions."

Her indecisive eyes riveted between mine.

"She's gonna let you in," Kyler whispered beside me.

Mrs. Fletcher stepped back and held the door open for me as Sue disappeared down the hall. Kyler followed me inside. Mrs. Fletcher closed the door and stared at me, her eyes drifting over my jeans and lavender hoodie. "What do you need to tell me about my son?"

"Can we maybe sit down?" I asked.

"Ask if my dad's here," Kyler said.

"Is your husband here? This concerns him too," I explained.

"Brad," she called as she walked me to the sitting room. "We have a visitor."

His footsteps creaked on the stairs as he descended from upstairs. He stepped into the room looking much like Kyler, only older with a light dusting of grey hair. "Hello," he said.

"Dad," Kyler whispered beside me.

I moved to the overstuffed gray loveseat and sat. Kyler sat beside me.

"This girl said she needs to speak with us," Mrs. Fletcher explained as they sat down opposite me on the matching sofa.

"Nora. My name's Nora," I said, my hands wringing together nervously in front of me.

"You got this," Kyler assured me.

"What can we do for you?" Mr. Fletcher asked.

"There's no real easy way to say this, so I'm just gonna say it and hope you don't kick me out," I said in one breath.

They both stared at me with narrowed eyes.

"Keep going," Kyler urged.

"I'm a medium," I said.

Mrs. Fletcher rolled her eyes as Mr. Fletcher crossed his arms.

"I speak to people's loved ones on the other side."

Mrs. Fletcher scoffed.

"I only ever see spirits who have passed, so you can understand my shock when your son came to me."

Mrs. Fletcher jumped to her feet. "That's enough! Get out!"

My stomach dropped. I'd already blown it.

Mr. Fletcher's hand shot out and he seized her wrist. "Sit down, honey. She came to talk to us and we're going to let her talk."

A sigh of relief escaped my lips. "Thank you."

Mrs. Fletcher begrudgingly sat back down, though her arms were crossed as she glared across the room at me.

"We've been through a lot," Mr. Fletcher explained.

"I understand. I would never lie about something like this. It's my job to bring messages to families, and I take that job very seriously," I explained.

"You said Kyler visited you?" he asked.

"He's here right now," I said.

"Ohmigod. That's it!" Mrs. Fletcher jumped to her feet again.

"Tell her I broke the window when I was seven and we kept it from my dad," Kyler said.

"He broke a window when he was seven and you kept it from Mr. Fletcher," I repeated.

She stilled.

"And tell her she used to call me her beautiful little boy even when I was in high school," Kyler said.

"You used to call him your beautiful little boy even when he was in high school," I said.

Her eyes glazed with tears.

"He's sitting right next to me," I explained. "He's been with me for a while now because he can't seem to go anywhere without me to assist him."

"Tell him to wake up," Mrs. Fletcher cried.

"He wants to," I explained. "He just doesn't know how to."

She lowered herself back down on the sofa. "Where is he?"

I looked to my right. "Right here. He's in a black hoodie and jeans."

"He was wearing that the night of the accident," Mr. Fletcher said.

"I want to feel him," Mrs. Fletcher said.

Kyler stood and walked in front of her, squatting to his haunches and touching her hands.

"He's touching your hands right now," I explained.

"I can't feel him," she said, tears trailing down her cheeks.

"I'm sorry. I wish you could."

He removed his hands from hers and touched his dad's hands.

"He's touching your hands right now, Mr. Fletcher," I explained.

He stared down at his hands but it was clear he couldn't feel Kyler either.

"Tell them I love them," Kyler said, standing up and moving back to the loveseat beside me.

"He loves you both very much," I explained.

Mr. Fletcher lifted his hands to his eyes and wiped away tears. "Will he ever wake up?"

"He doesn't know."

Mrs. Fletcher leaned into her husband and he wrapped his arm around her.

"Something happened the night of the accident," I explained. "He just can't seem to remember. We're not sure if he'll wake once he remembers or…"

The unspoken word hung heavy in the room.

"Has he seen himself?" Mrs. Fletcher asked through her tears.

I nodded. "He even thought he'd somehow be able to leap back into his body, like in the movies."

"And?" they both asked.

"It didn't work. It was like something was stopping him from getting close to himself."

A long stretch of silence passed between us. They were likely grappling with the idea that their son was in their living room even though they couldn't see him. And, I was waiting on them to accept the fact that as far-fetched as it seemed, this was their new reality if they wanted to communicate with him.

"He wanted to see you," I explained, breaking the silence in the room. "He wanted you to know he's still here."

Mrs. Fletcher covered her face with her palms and sobs tore out of her. "I miss him so much."

I looked to Kyler whose eyes had glazed over. He rose and moved beside his mom, wrapping his arms around her. My eyes cast down. It was difficult to know this was as close as he might ever get to being with his parents again.

"Is he in pain?" Mr. Fletcher asked.

I shook my head. "They don't feel pain in their spirit form."

"How can he be a spirit when he's not…" Mrs. Fletcher couldn't bring herself to say the word. "When he hasn't crossed over."

"I still see him the way I see other spirits," I explained.

"Except for the glow," Kyler said as if that made him different from the rest.

"Can he hear us when we speak to him?" Mr. Fletcher asked.

"The spirit version in this room can hear everything. But the one in the other room can't."

"So, we've wasted our time speaking to him?" Mrs. Fletcher asked.

"I don't think so. From everything I've read, it's important to keep their brains stimulated with words and music," I said.

"Tell my mom I miss her lasagna," Kyler said.

"He misses your lasagna."

She laughed and sniffled at the same time.

"Tell my dad I miss our football talks after my games."

I looked to Mr. Fletcher. "He misses your football talks after his games."

He shared a sad smile. "Tell him I do too."

"He can hear you," I assured him, my eyes cutting to Kyler who was still beside his mom.

"May I go see him?" I asked, wanting to leave the three of them alone.

"Of course," Mr. Fletcher said.

"He's sitting with you on the sofa right now. I'm gonna give you both some time to say whatever you need to say to him. I know he wants to hear it." I stood and looked to Kyler who shot me an appreciative smile. "If you need me to tell them anything, just come and get me."

"Thanks," he said.

I left them alone and walked into the first-floor bedroom. Kyler lay in bed exactly as he had the last time I was there. The ventilator still lifted his chest to give the impression that he was breathing on his own.

I lowered myself into the bedside chair, hating seeing this version of him. I took his hand from under the sheet and held it, wishing the gesture would awaken something in him. "Hi there…it would be awesome if you could just sit up and speak right now. Could you do that for me?" I paused, in case he did. He didn't. "The other you is with your parents right now. I hope they're telling you everything they've been telling this version of you…"

I glanced around the sterile room. There was a framed photo of Kyler and Melanie that hadn't been there last time. They were at a party and his arm was wrapped around her. Her smile beamed and it was easy to see the love she had for him. He, however, looked less excited. His smile was more forced. She definitely brought the photo over after seeing me there.

"You don't have to cross over." I squeezed his hand. "You can wake up. I'm just starting to get used to you hanging around…you're actually one of the better roommates I've had. You don't leave a mess. You don't eat all our food…and you're a good snuggler."

"Am I?" Kyler asked from the doorway.

I glanced to him. "How are they doing?"

He shrugged before stepping into the room. "They miss me."

"Obviously."

"They want me to wake up."

"We all do," I said. "Is there anything you want me to tell them for you?"

He stared down at his other self and shook his head. "I don't want it to be any harder on them."

"It's meant to comfort them," I said.

He didn't respond. His eyes latched onto the photo by his bedside. "What the hell?"

I laughed. "She wants to be with you."

"But I don't want to be with her." He winced, and I could see the look of pain cross over his face as he grabbed the sides of his head and doubled over.

"Kyler!" I jumped to my feet and leaned over with him, my hand on his back. "What's wrong?"

He didn't respond, just shook his head with his hands grasping it.

"You're scaring me. What's happening?"

"I don't know," he groaned.

"Jesus Christ! Tell me what to do," I pleaded.

He took a step back and dropped down into the chair. His hands remained on his head, but he used his knees to brace his elbows.

I rubbed his back, trying to soothe him. "You're gonna be okay."

He slowly lowered his hands, his breath coming out labored. He grabbed my hand, clutching it like a lifeline. "I'm scared."

I crawled onto his lap, holding him while he held me back. "I'm right here. I'm not going anywhere. What happened?"

"I don't know. A sharp pain just exploded in my head."

"Does it still hurt?"

"Just a dull ache now," he said.

"What set it off?" I asked.

"Stepping in here? Talking about Melanie?"

"Do you think a memory was coming back to you?"

"Like I didn't want to remember it?" he asked.

"She *is* keeping a secret," I reminded him.

"Nora?" Mr. Fletcher said from the doorway.

I sprang up quickly, knowing I must've looked strange curled up on the chair talking to myself.

Mr. Fletcher's eyes moved to the chair. I could see Kyler as clear as day, but I knew he couldn't. "Is he in here?"

I nodded, feeling like I'd been caught doing something I probably shouldn't be doing.

"We want him to know he's welcome here. He can even stay in his old room," he offered.

I looked to Kyler who sat up, the sadness in his eyes heartbreaking. He shook his head.

I looked back to his dad. "I don't think he can. He couldn't get in your house until I came in. He'd been trying before he found me. But once I was allowed in, he was too. I know it sounds crazy since…" my eyes drifted to the Kyler in the bed. "…he's already here."

Mr. Fletcher nodded. "I'm happy he found you."

"Me too," Kyler said.

I shot him a small smile before looking to his dad. "I am too. He's a great guy."

"The girls always loved him," Mr. Fletcher said as if he was no longer there.

But he *was* there. He was *right* there.

"So I've been told," I said.

"*Heeey*," Kyler admonished.

I smirked in his direction before looking to his dad. "What can you tell me about Melanie?"

"She's here every day. She's become like family."

My stomach roiled. "Does she ever talk about that night?"

He shook his head. "She said she wants to forget it."

"That's understandable," I said. "But she's never mentioned the events leading up to the accident?"

He shook his head. "Why? Has Kyler said anything?"

"No, he can't remember. But I spoke to his friend Bono. He said Kyler was going to break up with her when they left that party."

"She never told us that," he said.

"Told us what?" Mrs. Fletcher asked as she stepped into the doorway.

"That Kyler planned to break up with Melanie," Mr. Fletcher explained.

She shook her head. "I knew he wasn't that interested in her, but he never said anything about breaking up with her. And, as far as Melanie's concerned, they're going to get married when he wakes up."

Kyler laughed sardonically. "Never happening."

I looked to him. "Never say never."

"What's he saying?" Mrs. Fletcher asked.

"He said that's not happening."

"Tell them I've got my eye on someone else," Kyler said.

I cocked my head at him, trying not to melt in front of them.

"What?" Mrs. Fletcher pried.

"He said…"

"Go on," Kyler prompted.

I rolled my eyes. "He said he has his eye on someone else."

The Fletchers exchanged a knowing look.

Kyler burst into laughter. "I can't believe you actually told them."

"You told me to," I argued.

"What?" Mr. Fletcher asked.

I shook my head. "Your son is maddening."

They both smiled, though the smiles didn't reach their eyes. I couldn't imagine not being able to see someone I loved so much when they were standing right beside me.

I inched toward the door. "I should probably head out."

"Will you come back?" Mrs. Fletcher asked, though I knew she was really asking if I would bring Kyler back.

"Of course," I said.

"Great," she sighed.

I walked toward the front door with Kyler at my side. I could hear his parents on my heels. I stopped and turned to look at them. "Thanks again for letting me in."

Mrs. Fletcher caught me off guard and wrapped me in a hug. "Thank *you* for bringing our son home."

I didn't move, letting her hug me for as long as she needed to. This was such a stark contrast to the reception I'd received from her previously.

She released me as Mr. Fletcher nodded his appreciation. "Thank you for coming by." He opened the front door and Melanie stood there, her eyes widening when she spotted me with the Fletchers. "What's *she* doing here?" she asked, her jawline ticking.

I wish I could say my eyes stayed on hers, but they were on the old man standing behind her. The one who was with her at the café. The one I desperately needed to talk to.

CHAPTER 14

"Oh, Melanie. Hi," Mr. Fletcher said, quickly stepping back to let her inside their home.

"Nice to see you, *Lanie*," I said, crossing my arms and enjoying her surprise.

"Nora was just visiting Kyler," Mrs. Fletcher explained.

"She's hiding a secret," the old man now standing beside her said as if I hadn't caught it the last time we'd interacted.

"What?" I asked him point blank.

Everyone looked at me.

"*What* a coincidence that we meet again," I said, hoping that got the attention off me.

"It's my boyfriend's house. I'm always here," Melanie said.

"I thought you were heading to Boston for the holiday?" Mrs. Fletcher asked.

"I'm leaving in the morning," Melanie explained. "I needed to see Kyler before I left. And, have one more of your amazing dinners."

The old man behind her cocked his head as if trying to convey a message.

I needed to speak with him. I couldn't leave until I understood his message. "Now that you mention it, I'm pretty hungry myself. Will you be eating soon?" I asked Mrs. Fletcher.

"Oh, I…sure," she said confused by my sudden decision to stay.

"Great!" I said, way too excited over a meal.

Irritation flittered across Melanie's face. "I'm going to sit with Kyler." She spun away from us and walked down the hallway with her spirit in tow.

I looked quickly to Mrs. Fletcher and whispered, "I'm sorry to invite myself to dinner like that, but she's got a spirit with her who is trying to tell me something."

"Oh, dear," she said.

"I just need more time with her spirit," I explained.

"Well then, let me go make some dinner," Mrs. Fletcher said loudly enough for Melanie to hear before whispering to me, "Do whatever you need to do." She grasped her husband's arm and they walked into the kitchen.

"He's back?" Kyler asked me.

"You can't see him?"

He shook his head. "Is he talking?"

"He said the same thing," I whispered.

"Go in there. Tell Melanie you can see me. Tell her *I* said she's keeping a secret," Kyler urged.

"That could work," I agreed.

"It has to work," he said.

I turned toward the room, but he didn't move. "Are you coming?"

Uncertainty filled his face. "I don't think I should go back in there just yet."

"Yeah, I understand. I can handle it alone." I moved down the hallway and found Melanie in the chair at Kyler's bedside holding his hand.

"Why are you here?" she asked before I even stepped into the room.

"Because I had a message for the Fletchers," I said from the doorway.

She glanced over her shoulder at me. "Do you have a message for me too?" she asked condescendingly.

"Actually, Kyler is here," I said.

A small huff of laughter spilled out of her. "And let me guess. He's the ghost of Christmas past?"

I walked over so I could see her face when I delivered the news. "Nope. He said you're hiding something. A big secret about that night."

I watched her face falter for a split second before she recovered. "A secret?" she asked dubiously.

The old man stood in the corner of the room and nodded—liking my approach.

"One you don't want anyone to know," I added.

"Like what? I was carrying his baby?"

"What the hell?" Kyler said from the doorway.

"Um, no," I said. "Were you?"

"No," she said as if she would have liked that to be the truth.

"I think we both know what was going to happen when the two of you left the party together," I said, using what Bono had told me.

"I have no idea what you're talking about," she said.

"You wouldn't let Kyler break up with you before he left for school," I said.

Her face fell and I could see she was starting to realize he *was* there. "Did he tell you that?"

I nodded.

"Yeah, well, I knew he was making a rash decision that he wasn't sure of," she snapped.

I glanced to Kyler, not sure how much he wanted me to push. He nodded, urging me on. "That's not what he's saying," I continued.

"What *is* he saying exactly?" she challenged.

"You gave him the okay to see other girls at school, but when he got home you wanted to be with him."

She scoffed.

"And, the night of the party, he wasn't paying you any attention. You knew he was gonna break up with you when you left the party."

Her jaw tensed. She knew I was right.

"She caused the accident," Kyler said, the words a memory rushing back to him.

I sucked in a sharp breath, wishing I'd been wrong about her secret. "She did?"

"What's he saying?" she asked, having no clue of the severity of what he'd just revealed.

"She flipped out when I told her we were done. She said if she couldn't have me, no one would. Then she grabbed the wheel and I lost control. We crashed off the side of the bridge," he said, pain plaguing his features. "It felt like we were falling forever before we hit the water. I remember bracing for impact and then everything went black."

"Oh my God," I said, watching his despair.

"What?!" Melanie demanded.

"When I came to," he continued. "I knew I needed to get her out first since she was screaming. But, once I got her free, my seatbelt was stuck. I couldn't get out. I was trapped. I had no air. I tried. God, I tried. But my air ran out and…everything disappeared."

"What's he saying?!" she demanded again.

My eyes cut back to hers. "*You* caused the accident."

"What are you talking about?" she snapped.

"You said no one was gonna have him if you couldn't. So, you grabbed the steering wheel and Kyler lost control of the car," I said.

"Prove it," she snarled.

"I don't have to prove it. I know the truth. And Kyler knows the truth. When he wakes up, he'll confirm it."

She sprang to her feet and moved within inches of my face. I braced myself for a slap. But she only leaned in seething. "I don't know what you've got going on with my boyfriend, but don't fuck with me." A scary smile spread across her face. "I'd hate to trip over one of these wires." Her eyes moved to the ones attached to the machines keeping Kyler alive.

The hair on the back of my neck stood on end. I didn't doubt her words. She'd grabbed the wheel and put Kyler in the situation he was currently in. But the truth remained. I couldn't prove it. I had the word of two spirits. And, she could pull the plug on him at any time.

She stood back up, straightening out her shirt that had wrinkled in her attempt to intimidate me. She said nothing as she walked out of the room with her spirit following her.

I turned to look at Kyler with wide eyes. "She's insane."

He slid down the wall until he was sitting with his knees bent and his face buried in his arms.

I rushed over to him and sat beside him, rubbing my hand gently over his back. "Is it happening again?"

He didn't respond.

"Jesus, Kyler. Are you okay?"

He didn't respond.

"Kyler, look at me," I said, urging his arms away from his face. "Are you all right?"

"She did this."

"We'll make sure she's punished."

He scoffed. "How?"

"I don't know…."

"What good does knowing the truth do us?" he asked, frustration dripping from his words.

I hated that I didn't have the answer. That I couldn't make it all better.

"Everything okay in here?" Mr. Fletcher asked from the doorway.

"What makes you ask?" I said from the floor, knowing how strange I must've looked down there.

His thumb hitched behind him. "Melanie just stormed out claiming she didn't feel well."

I stood up. "I don't doubt that." I glanced to Kyler who read my thoughts and nodded his consent. I looked back to Mr. Fletcher. "She caused Kyler's accident."

His head tilted to the side. "Come again?"

"Kyler remembered everything," I explained.

"Jesus Christ," he said, shocked.

"I'm so sorry to tell you like this, but we just found out and she knows we know," I said.

"What's going on?" Mrs. Fletcher asked, appearing in the doorway.

"Melanie caused Ky's accident," Mr. Fletcher explained.

Her stunned eyes jumped to mine. "What?!"

I nodded. "Kyler remembered."

"He remembered?" she asked.

"Everything," I assured her. "Melanie grabbed the wheel and he lost control."

"That *bitch*!" she cursed, seething with hate. "How dare she come into our home? How dare she play the victim *knowing* she did this to our baby?"

"What do we do now?" Mr. Fletcher asked me.

"Don't let her back in here. She threatened to tamper with his machines if I told anyone," I said.

Mrs. Fletcher gasped. "We need to call the police."

"And tell them what?" I asked, knowing that wouldn't work.

"Well, what you just told us," she said.

"I think we all know they won't take my word on this. Most people think mediums are frauds."

I watched as my words hit close to home as Mrs. Fletcher definitely thought I was one when I arrived.

"Was there a detective associated with the case after the accident?" I asked.

"Only at first when they weren't sure if it had been a hit and run," Mr. Fletcher explained.

"Can you call them?" I asked. "You know, see if anything seemed out of the ordinary that night?"

"We all assumed it was ice," Mrs. Fletcher said, her voice low like she still couldn't believe this accident wasn't really an accident. Melanie had purposely done this. Done this because Kyler didn't want her.

"It wouldn't hurt to call and plant the seed that you have doubts," I said.

Mr. Fletcher pulled his phone from his pocket. "I'll do that right now."

"At least you won't have to worry about Melanie while she's in Boston," I said, my eyes jumping between the Fletchers. "And hopefully we'll have some answers or evidence before she gets back."

"Can we get out of here?" Kyler asked, pushing himself to his feet.

I looked at him. He'd been so quiet, I'd almost forgotten he was there. "Are you okay?"

He shrugged.

"What is it?" Mrs. Fletcher asked.

"I think it's been a lot on him today," I explained.

"Does he need anything?" she asked, clearly wanting to fix it.

My look conveyed her question to Kyler.

"I just need to hold you tonight," he said to me.

My stomach dipped. The feeling was mutual. "He's just tired," I explained to his parents. "We're gonna head out."

"Thank you for helping him," Mrs. Fletcher said as she walked me out of the room. Kyler and Mr. Fletcher followed us to the front door.

Mr. Fletcher stepped forward and opened the door for me. "You're a godsend, Nora."

I forced a smile.

"Thank you, Nora," Mrs. Fletcher said. "We owe you the world."

I stepped outside, feeling as though I didn't deserve their praise. I was just doing what I always did—giving comfort to those who needed it. I just never expected to stumble upon such a bombshell in the process.

"So that went well," Kyler said once we were back in my car still parked out front.

I laughed nervously because I wasn't sure whether to laugh or cry. "Are you okay?"

"Yeah…" He leaned over and cupped one of my cheeks with his hand, his fingertips gliding gently over my skin like he was memorizing my features. "…because of you." He pressed his lips to mine and, at that moment, his kiss was all I needed.

I pulled away first and assessed his tired eyes. "What do we do now?"

"We go home," he said, even though he knew that wasn't what I meant.

"You sure?" I asked.

"There's a lot I'm not sure about. And this is not one of them," he assured me.

CHAPTER 15

Izzy's car wasn't in the driveway when we returned to my house. Kyler headed straight for the stairs. I followed, eager to be alone with him after the trying day we'd had.

There was a knock on the front door.

"What the hell?" Kyler grumbled.

I stopped and moved to the door. Once I pulled it open, Rick stood there staring at me with glazed red eyes.

Dammit.

"What about our last conversation made you think you could just show up here?" I began to close the door but his hand shot out and stopped it.

"I need to talk to you," he said with a slur in his voice as he pushed his way unsteadily inside my living room.

"Jesus Christ," Kyler huffed, coming back down the stairs.

I looked to him, just as confused as him by Rick's drunken intrusion.

"What'd you just do?" Rick said, his words slurred. "Is one of your ghosts here?"

"Spirits. And yes. So, you can leave," I said.

"Why won't you hear me out?" he growled.

"There's nothing to hear."

"Yes, there is. I love you, Nora. I want you back and you're making this so damn difficult."

"This guy's completely lost his mind," Kyler said, crossing his arms and eyeing him like a hawk.

"I don't love you, Rick," I assured him.

"How can you even say that? We were together for a year. A fucking *year*, Nora. That's got to mean something."

"It didn't mean anything to you when you cheated on me," I said.

Rage flared in his eyes. "Fuck you."

My head hitched back. "Excuse me?"

"When are you gonna get over that? It was clearly a mistake."

There was no talking sense to a drunk Rick. I glanced to Kyler who looked ready to pounce. I held up my hand to let him know I'd handle it. I walked to the door and jerked it open. "You need to leave, Rick."

He huffed his annoyance as he staggered toward the door, but instead of walking out, he ripped my hand away from the knob with such vigor it threw me off balance and launched me halfway across the living room.

Kyler sprang, his fists coming from both sides as he pummeled Rick with blow after blow to his head. I'd never seen this rage in Kyler, and I wondered if part of it stemmed from his recollections of the accident.

"What the fuck?" Rick screamed as "an invisible force" took him to the ground, relentless with its fists. Blood poured from Rick's nose as he used his arms to protect himself from the unseen attacker.

"Kyler," I said, pulling at the back of his hoodie to get him off of Rick. "He's not worth it."

Kyler landed a few more blows before climbing off of him.

Rick, clasping his bloody nose, sprang to his feet with fear in his eyes as he searched my living room for the entity that had just beaten his ass. The entity that only I could see who was currently breathing heavily and staring at me. "What was *that?*"

Good question. As far as I knew, Kyler could only touch *me*. "That was your cue to get out of here and never come back," I said.

He rushed to the door and stumbled outside. I slammed the door and locked it, overwhelmed by his aggression with me *and* Kyler's reaction to it.

"I'm not sorry," Kyler said before I even turned around.

When I did, he stood with his hands in his pockets. I took the two steps necessary to stand in front of him and removed his hands from his pockets, examining his knuckles. "Are you hurt?"

He smirked. "No, but he is."

I cocked my head. "You didn't need to do that."

"He wasn't gonna lay a hand on my girl," he said.

I sucked in a sharp breath as butterflies swarmed in my belly.

"Now, he'll never be back," he assured me.

I slipped my fingers into his. "Did any of that have to do with Melanie?"

He shrugged.

"I wouldn't blame you if it did," I said, my thumbs rubbing gently over the backs of his hands.

"I never imagined she had it in her. I knew she was whacked-out, but to purposely try to kill me…that's some messed up shit."

I said nothing because he needed to say this. He needed to process it.

"She needs to pay," he said. "She's taken everything from me."

He was right. The only positive to come from the accident was us meeting, and I knew, without a shadow of a doubt, he'd sacrifice that to have his life back. "You need to wake up and tell someone."

His lips twisted regrettably. That was the only way to have definitive proof. But, currently, that didn't help us.

"Do you think she confided in any of her friends?" I asked.

"Would you if you did something so horrific?" he asked.

"I'm not her," I said. "So, there's no telling what a crazy person would do."

He dropped his forehead to mine. "I have no idea what I would've done if I didn't meet you."

I smiled a sad smile knowing that the circumstances that brought us together sucked.

"I'm not your ex, Nora. I'd never lay a hand on you or betray you," he began. "I'm just scared that no matter how all of this ends, I'll hurt you."

"You'd never purposely hurt me. I know that."

He pulled back just enough to see my eyes. His riveted between them. "Do you?"

I nodded.

He released our hands and slipped his arms around my hips, pulling me against him. "When you're around, everything just makes sense."

The rush of emotions flooding my body wouldn't allow me to speak. I wanted to smile at the vulnerability in his words but cry at the inevitability of our fate.

"Am I selfish for not wanting to lose you despite knowing this could all end really badly?"

I slipped my arms over his shoulders, needing to be closer to him. "It's my decision too, you know. I do get a say in all this."

"Have I left you a say, or have I just relied on you without asking permission?"

"I've told you before. I want to help you."

"Help me? Or be with me?"

I swallowed down the lump in my throat wondering what I had to lose for admitting the truth. "Both."

A small smile pulled at the corners of his mouth. "Tomorrow isn't promised to anyone."

"I know."

"I want all your tomorrows, Nora. And I want you to have all of mine," he said. "And if that makes me a selfish prick. I'll own that." He didn't let me respond. His mouth sealed over mine, his tongue pushing between my lips and holding me a willing captive.

He lifted me off my feet causing me to wrap my legs around his hips. He didn't stop kissing me as he climbed the stairs and walked straight to my room. He lay me down on my bed and followed me down, covering me with his body. His erection pressed between my thighs and fire erupted inside me, spreading over my body. I'd never wanted anyone as much as I wanted him in this moment.

My hands slipped around his hips, burrowing under his T-shirt and hoodie. My fingertips slid over the soft skin on his back, tracing figure-eights the length of it. They eventually moved to his hips and slipped around until they grasped the button on his jeans. "Stop trying to get me naked," he said against my lips.

"You *are* the streaker," I chuckled as I kept at it, slipping the button through the slot.

"I'm serious," he said, pulling back enough to look me in the eyes. "I expect nothing."

"Well then, you are going to be pleasantly surprised."

He sighed, knowing I wasn't stopping and he couldn't deny me this. He lifted his weight off me and let me push his jeans down his legs. Once they reached his feet, he kicked off his shoes and jeans but left his boxers on.

"Oh no," I said, feeling brave. "Those too."

His brows shot up. "You sure?"

"I've never been more sure," I said, knowing this is what it was supposed to feel like when it was right.

He nodded, as if he could read my thoughts, then pushed his boxers off.

I kept my eyes on his, though it took everything in me not to look down.

"Why am I always the naked one?" he chuckled.

I reached around and unhooked my bra, then lifted my arms over my head. He tugged my shirt and bra off. I kept my eyes on his. He didn't look down, though I knew the desire was there. He leaned down and pressed his lips to mine, slow and intentional. This meant something to him. I was offering myself to him this way when I'd never been ready to do it before. He wasn't going to rush this. He was going to make it memorable and special. He pulled away from my lips and peppered my neck with open-mouthed kisses. "Do you trust me?"

"Yes," I sighed.

"I would never do anything that you didn't want to do," he said.

"I know," I whispered.

"Do you know how much you mean to me?"

"I'm starting to see."

"Starting to see?" he asked incredulously. "Then you better let me show you." His hand slipped down between us. He unsnapped my jeans, sliding them down my legs with my panties. Knowing he wouldn't get them past my shoes, I pushed them off my feet. He slid my clothes the rest of the way off and tossed them to the floor. "You good?" he asked, his eyes zeroed in on mine.

I nodded, feeling his erection pressed to my stomach. "We need a condom," I said.

"I'm not sure it works like that when I'm not really…well…" He let the rest of his thought linger in the air.

I closed my eyes, forgetting that while all of this was so real to me, he was right. He was in that bedroom back home with his parents.

"Hey," he said. I opened my eyes and he was right there. "I'm here."

I nodded.

He leaned down, kissing me in a way that reminded me that if all of this ended tomorrow, I'd have this memory. These feelings. This night. And no one could take it away from me. He slowly started to grind his hips against mine, letting me adjust to the idea of what was about to happen. His erection slipped between my legs, the shaft gliding over my folds. I pulled in a breath.

"You okay?" he asked.

"Perfect," I assured him and I meant it. I wasn't scared. I wasn't uncomfortable. I was ready. I shifted my hips, lifting them to meet his.

He reached down and adjusted the tip, gliding it over my folds, back and forth. "Lift your knees," he urged.

I did, cradling him between them.

He balanced on his forearms his eyes locked on mine. "Ready?"

I nodded.

He gently thrust his hips forward, the tip pushing slightly inside me. He paused, giving me time to adjust before thrusting forward again. This time the tip drove in a little deeper. He paused again before driving a little deeper. "You ready?" he asked.

I nodded, knowing I wanted this with him so damn much.

"I've got you," he assured me.

"I know," I whispered.

He leaned down and captured my lips as he thrust all the way inside of me. I released a soft groan as I took all of him. It wasn't painful, just full. He didn't pull out, letting me adjust to the length of him inside of me as he continued to kiss me. He eventually pulled out, driving back in deeper still. He groaned this time, and I pulled away from his lips, needing to catch my breath. I felt him everywhere.

His lips found my neck as my head fell back. My breathing was labored as he continued thrusting. "You're beautiful," he said between kisses to my skin.

I sighed.

"And you feel fucking amazing," he said against my neck.

I hummed my appreciation.

"Does this feel good for you?" he asked.

My hands slipped around to his ass, answering his question by urging him deeper.

He chuckled softly and obliged.

The slapping of our bodies was the only sound in my room as all the sensations began to coil between my thighs. "Oh, God," I groaned.

"Are you close?" he asked, burying his lips in the crook of my neck.

"Yes," I breathed.

He thrust faster, his ass between my hands moving with vigor.

My insides tightened. He reached down and his thumb brushed my clit. A burst of sensation released in waves out to every part of my body, tremors rippling in the wake and shooting every which way. I could barely catch my breath as he locked his hands beside my head and thrust harder still. He followed me over the edge with a long, drawn-out groan before lowering himself down on top of me. The weight of him pressed me to the bed, and it felt so damn right. As if this was meant to be.

Our heavy breathing was the only sound in the room. I savored the moment knowing I could hear breath no one else could hear. I could feel touch no one else could feel. I could listen to words meant for no one else but me.

Kyler lifted his head and stared down at me, pushing sweaty pieces of my hair away from my forehead. "You okay?"

"Very."

He met me with a slow-spreading smile before wrapping his arms around me. He stayed inside of me for a long time, just holding me like something precious. Something he had no plans of letting go of. "So, was it worth waiting for?"

"It was worth waiting for with *you*."

He smiled, pressing his lips to mine in a quick chaste kiss. "I need to get you cleaned up," he said as he eased himself up and pulled out of me slowly. The loss of him inside of me left me feeling bereft. I didn't realize the experience would forge such a connection. One that couldn't easily be broken. Kyler stopped, his contemplative eyes narrowing.

"What's wrong?" I asked.

"I can't pick up a towel," he said.

"What?"

"I can touch you and things related to you. I could punch the asshole because ultimately the rage had to do with him touching you. But, actually picking something up, I haven't mastered that trick yet." He looked upset with himself for not realizing that.

"I'm a big girl. I can take care of myself." I slipped out from under him and grabbed my pajamas from my drawer on my way to the bathroom. There was no blood when I washed myself, and I wondered if everything that happened had *actually* happened. Because in my mind, and in my body, I knew I very much experienced all of it.

I returned a few minutes later to find Kyler under my comforter.

His eyes drifted over my purple booty shorts and matching tank. "You're gorgeous without clothes, but I'm kinda diggin' you in your pajamas."

I rolled my eyes and climbed under the comforter. Kyler wrapped his arms around me as I snuggled into his chest.

"Can I ask you something?" he said.

"Of course."

"Will you come with me to my parents' for Christmas Eve?"

I laughed. "That's what you want to know right now?"

"Would you prefer I ask how I performed?" he asked.

"Um, no."

"Well, then. What do you say? Will you come with me to my parents' house?"

"Most awkward dinner ever."

"Probably. But it would mean a lot to me."

I considered a witty comeback, but his sincerity deserved the truth. "Then, yes. I'd love to."

CHAPTER 16

"I land at ten, so we'll be able to spend all Christmas day together," my mom assured me as I talked to her on my way to work.

"I can't wait."

"What will you do on Christmas Eve?" she asked as I maneuvered around groups of shoppers jamming up the sidewalk.

"Um…"

"*Um?* What does *um* mean?" she asked.

"It means…I kind of have plans," I said.

"With Izzy?"

Here goes nothing. "I'm kind of seeing…someone."

"What?!" she screeched so loudly I had to pull the phone away from my ear. "Why is this the first I'm hearing of this?"

"It all just sort of happened," I explained.

"Tell me everything. What's his name?"

"Kyler."

"I like that name. Where'd you meet? Don't tell me one of those dating apps."

I laughed. "No. I met him at…work." It wasn't a total lie.

"So? What's he like?"

"Well…he's gorgeous. And funny. And, he treats me well."

"Oh, thank God. I've been so worried about you since what that asshole Rick did. I'm so happy you finally moved on."

"I have."

"Will I meet Kyler on Christmas?"

"Oh…" I reached the alley between the buildings and hurried to the café's back door. "I'm not sure. Maybe…Actually…Probably not."

"Nora? You're acting weird. What aren't you telling me? Are your readings getting to be too much for you? Talk to me."

"Mom, I just got to the café," I said, stepping inside the back room. "I'm gonna have to call you later."

"As soon as your shift is over," she demanded.

"Fine." I disconnected the call, knowing I was safe from any more of her questions—at least for the next six hours.

I pulled off my coat and grabbed my apron from the hook, tying it behind my back as I walked out front.

"Hey, glad you're here!" Daci said.

I noticed the long line of customers snaking its way to the door. "Hey," I said as I hurried to the register to wait on the next customer. That's when I noticed Kyler was there, seated at a table watching me.

I couldn't stop thinking about last night. There were so many emotions running through me. Everything had been so perfect. Was he thinking the same thing? Feeling the same way?

"Nora?" Daci said.

I glanced over my shoulder.

"You okay? You just froze there for a minute."

"I'm fine," I said, turning back to the customer as Kyler laughed in the background.

* * *

After the lunch rush, I was able to take a break. I removed my apron and made my way over to the table where Kyler still sat. "You know, I don't need a bodyguard," I said like a ventriloquist trying not to move my lips.

"I know you don't."

"Well, then why have you been hanging out here all day?" I asked. "Aren't you bored?"

"Can't I just watch you work?"

"You can, but why would you want to?" I asked.

"People watch TV which is not nearly as interesting," he said, never missing a beat.

"Unless it's *The Hangover*," I reminded him.

"There's always an exception." He smiled. "Seriously, I'm here because I have a question for you."

"I knew there had to be more to it."

He laughed.

Daci stepped up to the table, her excitement palpable. "Is he here?"

Kyler looked to me with raised brows. "You told her about me?"

I closed my eyes for a beat before looking to Daci. "Yes."

Her wide eyes looked to Kyler, though I knew all she was looking at was an empty chair. "Hurt her and I hurt you," she warned.

I laughed, unprepared for her threat. I glanced around to see if any of the people seated at the nearby tables were watching this madness.

"I'll try not to," Kyler said, stifling a grin.

"He said he'd never hurt such a beautiful goddess," I relayed to Daci.

Daci smiled at the empty chair. "Smart guy."

"Wow, edit much?" Kyler asked me.

"I knew it's what you were thinking," I said.

The bell on the door jingled as a customer entered the café.

"Well," Daci said. "Keep doing whatever you're doing because I haven't seen Nora this happy in a long time."

"Goodbye, Daci," I urged.

She laughed before walking back to the counter to wait on the customer.

"So, I make you happy?" Kyler asked, kicking out his legs and crossing them at the ankles.

I cocked my head.

He laughed at my non-answer. "So, as I was saying before your lovely friend interrupted, I wanted to ask you to do something with me tonight."

"A date?" I asked.

"Yes, a date."

"Where will we go?"

"It's a surprise," he said.

"I like surprises," I assured him.

The bell jingled again and another customer entered the café. "I should get back to work," I whispered. "Are you picking me up here or at home?"

"I wish I could pick you up. But you're gonna have to settle for me picking you up at your bedroom door."

"What should I wear?"

"Something warm," he said.

"I can do that." I stood from the chair. "I'll see you tonight." I headed back to the counter. When I glanced over at Kyler's table, he'd already disappeared.

CHAPTER 17

"Knock, knock," Kyler said at my bedroom door. He hadn't been in the living room when I got home from work. I wondered if he was trying to give the impression of him picking me up for a date.

I opened the door. His eyes moved over my green turtleneck sweater, jeans, and boots. "Will I be warm enough?" I asked.

"Yeah, but grab your coat, a hat, and a blanket," he said.

"I'm not sure if you're aware, but I'm not an outdoorsy kind of girl."

He laughed as he swept out his arm, gesturing for me to go down the stairs before him.

"Izzy was here earlier," he said once we were downstairs. "She said to tell you she'd be home late."

"She told you that?"

"Well, she shouted it back into the house before she left. I guess she thought it was worth trying," he said.

I laughed as I grabbed my coat and hat from the living room closet and put them on. I reached back in and grabbed a red wool blanket and tucked it under my arm. "Are you gonna tell me where we're going?" I asked as we stepped outside.

"It's a surprise," he said, taking my hand and leading me to my car.

Once we were on the road, I could sense Kyler's eyes on me. "What?" I asked, my eyes jumping between him and the road.

"So, you caved and told Daci about me?"

"She saw Melanie leaving angry after her reading," I explained. "I had to tell her something."

"Does this make us official then?" he asked, his lips twitching wildly.

I shrugged. "Not sure. You haven't taken me to your parents' basement yet."

His brows shot up. "I didn't realize you were that kind of girl."

"Well, if it was good enough for your high school girls, I'm thinking it's good enough for me."

He chuckled, and I liked knowing I could bring that out of him.

After driving for another few minutes with Kyler giving me directions, I realized where he was taking me. Where he had the *nerve* to take me.

My eyes shot to his. "We're going to the beach?" I asked, unable to disguise my annoyance.

A smile slipped across his lips. "Turning a tragedy into a comedy?"

"Comedy?" I asked.

He laughed. "I don't know. What's the opposite of a tragedy?"

I thought for a minute. "I'm not really sure."

"See?"

The sign for the exit appeared up ahead, and I took the exit despite my reluctance. "Are we just driving by?" I asked with hope in my voice.

"Oh no. We're stopping," he said with a grin.

Within minutes, I'd pulled into the sandy lot and cut the engine. "Okay. We're here."

He ignored my pissy-ness and stepped out of the car. "Come on, scaredy cat."

"I'm not scared. I'm annoyed," I grumbled as I stepped out. I expected a salty breeze from the waves to whip my hair around my face, but the breeze was minimal—especially with my hat pulled down to my eyes.

Kyler met me at my door. "I want you to have good memories of the beach, not shitty ones."

I stared at him, my eyes roaming over his face. *That's why he brought me here?*

"What?" he asked, his brows slanted inward.

I shook my head. "Maybe I don't hate you after all."

"You hated me?"

I reached inside my backseat and grabbed the blanket, then closed the door. "Well, this seemed like a terrible idea. But now I understand." I leaned in and pressed my lips to his. "So, thank you."

"I haven't even shown you what we came for," he said, slipping his hand into mine. "Come on." He pulled me toward the beach.

Surrounded by darkness, we walked through the sand. Before I'd discovered Rick cheating with Zoe here, I'd only ever visited the beach in the daytime when the gulls were snatching food off the sand and the sun glistened off the water. But being here at night, brought on a whole different vibe. It was peaceful. And, it was all ours.

Kyler stopped. "Mind laying out the blanket?"

I shook it out into a perfect square on the sand.

Kyler urged me down until we sat side by side. "Lay back," he said as he took my hand in his again.

The waves crashed on the shore in rhythmic succession as I lay beside him completely at ease and content. Stars filled the sky like a real-life planetarium. It was exquisite.

With his free hand, he pointed up and traced the constellation with his finger. "That right there is Ursa Major also known as the Great Bear. If you look closely, the handle of the Big Dipper is the tail of the bear."

I squinted up and was able to pick out the tail of the bear in the sky. "How do you know that?"

"I took astronomy last year."

"I had no idea you were into astronomy."

"Full disclosure? I thought it was gonna be a class about people's signs. You know, Aries and Capricorn."

I laughed. "Astrology?"

"Yeah. Girls love that stuff."

"You took the class hoping to meet girls?"

He shrugged. "On the first day of class, I noticed there weren't that many girls in the class. Then, the professor started talking about constellations, and I realized my mistake."

I couldn't tell if he was lying or telling the truth, but it didn't matter. When I was around him, I was swept up in his good energy.

"Anyway," he continued, "it turned out to be fascinating stuff."

"Show me more."

He pointed to another section of the sky and traced another constellation. "Ursa Minor is the Little Dipper. It's distinguishable by the North Star at the end of the handle."

"Oh, I see it," I said, noting the brightest star at the end.

He moved his finger and pointed far off to the left. "That big one way over there is Orion. Follow my finger." He traced the constellation. "It's also called the Great Hunter because see right down at the bottom there? See the shape of the bow and arrow?"

I couldn't quite make out what he was explaining, but I loved his enthusiasm as he explained it.

"Am I boring you?" he asked.

"What? No. This is one of the best dates I've ever been on," I said.

"*One* of the best?" he asked.

"I recall a Christmas light adventure that ranks pretty high."

He rolled onto his side, resting his cheek in his palm. "Oh yeah?"

"You fishing for a compliment?"

His lips twitched. "Maybe."

I rolled onto my side to face him and smiled. "Best dates ever."

"Liar."

"Spirit."

He leaned forward and pressed his lips to mine. I wrapped my arms around him and pulled him on top of me, my lips moving desperately over his. He groaned deep in his throat and I thought he might want to take things further—since there was not another soul on the beach, but he eventually pulled back leaving me gasping for air and turned on beyond reason. He stood up and held his hand down to me.

I stared at it, confused by the change in direction.

"Come on."

I grasped it and he pulled me to my feet.

"Take out your phone and put on your favorite slow song," he explained.

I pulled out my phone and scrolled through a playlist. "Setting the mood?"

"Just giving you the full Kyler Fletcher high school experience."

Laughter tumbled out of me as I chose "Here With Me" by d4vd. Once it began to play, I tucked my phone into my coat pocket.

Kyler slipped his arms around to my back and pulled me against his chest. I draped my arms over his shoulders, and he swayed us in time to the music.

"Dancing under the stars," I said. "You're pulling out all the stops tonight."

"Only the best for you," he assured me.

"How many girls have you brought to the beach?" I asked.

"Only one."

Jealousy swirled inside me. "Who was she?"

He cocked his head. "Just some girl who doesn't know how extraordinary she is."

I stifled a grin.

"One who has my back no matter what," he continued.

A ripple rolled through my belly.

"One who'd take down anyone to protect me, including the blonde bitch who tried to kill me."

"I would."

"You would," he agreed, taking my hand and spinning me around.

I threw back my head and laughed, and there wasn't a thing in this world—or any other—that could stop it.

"Don't ever stop doing that," he said once he'd pulled me against him again.

"What?"

"Laughing. Smiling. Being amazing."

I slipped my arms back over his shoulders and stared into his pretty eyes. "Only if you agree first."

Sadness filled his eyes, and I knew he hated not being able to make that promise. "I'll try."

"I'll take that," I said, resting my head against his shoulder and letting him sway us to the music.

"So, how many guys have *you* danced with on a beach?" he asked.

"It's a long list," I said. "You sure you wanna know?"

"I think I can handle it," he said.

"Well…let me think…ummm…maybe the list isn't *that* long."

He chuckled.

"Now that I think about it, there was just one," I admitted.

"Who was he?" he asked, playing along.

"Just some guy who doesn't know how extraordinary *he* is."

"Go on," he said, fishing for compliments again.

"One who is too good looking for his own good," I continued.

"You think I'm—*he's* good looking?" he asked.

"Very. And he has this way of making me feel special."

"Has? Should I take that to mean you still see him?" he asked.

I pulled back and looked him in the eyes. "Oh, I see him."

His lips slipped into a sexy smile. "Is he a good dancer?"

"Very."

He laughed, and when he laughed like that, I really believed everything was going to be okay.

CHAPTER 18

"I don't like not knowing," Kyler said from the passenger seat of my car the next night.

The beams of my headlights cast a bright glow on the otherwise dark road. "You'll see," I said, hoping he enjoyed my plan for us.

"Is it a good surprise or a bad surprise?" he asked.

My eyes jumped between him and the road. I was excited that it was my turn to surprise him. "Good. I hope." He stared out the window and the closer we got to the destination, I wondered if he had any idea where we were headed.

His head whipped over his shoulder and he peered out the back window.

"What's wrong?"

"That car's been behind us the whole way."

I glanced in my rearview mirror noting the faint headlights from a car at least a hundred yards behind us. "I can assure you. They're not going where we are."

He twisted back around and looked at me. "And where was that again?"

I shook my head, enjoying his attempt to get me to reveal the surprise.

My GPS eventually instructed me to turn right up ahead.

"Wait," Kyler said, his head whipping around.

I laughed.

"Why are we going here?" he asked as the sign for his high school appeared.

"It's a surprise," I reminded him, hoping the storm clouds that had moved in held off long enough for me to actually surprise him.

I drove through the front entrance, past the falcon statue in the front of the building. I glanced in my rearview mirror just in time to see that the car that had been behind us did not pull into the school like we had. As I turned into the side parking lot, Kyler's eyes took in the campus.

"I haven't been back here since I graduated," he said.

I cut the engine and looked to him. "Show me around."

"Really?"

I nodded. "I want to see you in your element." I pushed open my door and by the time I stepped out, he was already at my side. He took my hand and walked me around the vacant campus pointing out everything from the outdoor cafeteria to the mural outside the art wing. Though darkness had already descended, we walked in no rush at all.

"Do you think we would've been friends in high school?" I asked.

"Friends? Yes."

"You wouldn't have wanted to date me?"

He contemplated my question. "You were probably too good for me."

"Nice one," I teased.

"No, I'm serious. My head was on one thing. I was a stupid guy. I would've blown it with you if I tried."

"And, I wouldn't have given it up, so there's that," I laughed.

"I told you. You would have for me."

I rolled my eyes and shoved him. "You're so stupid."

He laughed. "I just told you that, too."

We walked across the outdoor basketball court and over to the fence surrounding the football field. "Is this bringing back memories?"

"A little. Did I tell you I hold the school's record for the most touchdown receptions?"

"Really?"

"Yeah, it sounds better than it is. Our QB ended up at Alabama and then the pros. So, it was really about *his* arm. I just caught the passes."

"Have I heard of him?"

He shrugged. "Flip Caruso. He's a backup right now. But, he'll likely get a shot next year when their starter retires."

I stepped out onto the field. "Show me what you've got."

A few raindrops landed on my hoodie. I looked up at the darkening clouds, knowing they could open up at any moment. And, if I was going to go through with my plan, it was now or never.

"We don't have a ball," Kyler said unfazed by the rain. "*And*, I couldn't catch it if we did."

"That's not exactly what I meant."

His eyes narrowed as he watched me peel off my hoodie.

His head cocked to the side. "Nora?"

"I seem to recall a funny story Bono told me," I said, removing my shirt so that I was only in my bra.

"You wouldn't?" he said.

"You gonna join me?" I asked as my fingers unfastened the button on my jeans.

He laughed. "You're crazy."

"You did it first," I reminded him.

He seemed to consider it for a moment, then he reached behind his neck and tugged his hoodie and T-shirt over his head in one fluid motion.

I kicked off my sneakers and pushed my jeans down my legs so that I was only wearing my panties.

Kyler's eyes smoldered as they moved over my body. Then, he shoved off his sneakers and dropped his jeans.

I turned toward the end zone and took off running down the field. The once-soft blades of grass were a little sharper in December. I couldn't hear Kyler's footsteps behind me, but I knew he'd followed. He eventually caught up with me, wrapping his arms around my stomach from behind and lifting me right off my feet causing me to squeal.

"Did you really think I wouldn't catch you?" he asked against my ear.

Just then, the clouds opened up and rain poured down on us. I lifted my face to the sky and laughed while the rain soaked me to the bone. I couldn't picture a more perfect moment.

Kyler placed me down, spinning me to face him.

Raindrops hung from my eyelashes as I gazed up at him. "How did this feel with a crowd of people watching?" I asked.

"Not as good as it feels right now." He pushed wet strands of hair away from my face. "I'm glad I didn't meet you in high school."

I smirked. "I definitely wouldn't have gone streaking with you."

"No, but you would have been screaming with the other girls as I ran across this field."

"Probably. You're hot."

He laughed, and I wished I could always make him laugh like that. "I think we were meant to meet now."

"Yeah?"

He nodded, and the way he looked at me heated my shivering body to the core. And, though his words—and the notion—should have made me happy, a dull ache formed in my chest like an emptiness that needed to be filled. We both understood the curse of our timing, and the ticking clock hovering above us with every one of our breaths.

"Let's keep living in the moment," he said, noting the unease in my eyes. "Because those moments become our tomorrows. And, you promised me all of yours."

I smiled. "I did, didn't I?"

"You did." He smirked.

"And I'd never go back on a promise," I said, playing along.

He shook his head slowly as rain continued to fall. "You wouldn't."

"So, I guess—"

He didn't let me finish. His lips crashed down on mine, determined to show me that our timing wasn't ill-fated. He lifted me off the ground, and my bare legs wrapped around his hips. He never stopped kissing me, giving it all he had and then some as the rain continued to pour down upon us.

We had today.

And, that would lead to tomorrow.

Was anyone really promised more than that?

CHAPTER 19

I stood at my kitchen counter arranging the Christmas cookies I'd spent the last three hours baking on a platter.

"You need to be careful."

I froze. The male voice behind me wasn't Kyler's.

"You're getting in too deep."

Normally, the voice brought me comfort. Normally, I couldn't wait to see the smile on his face. But this time, I knew there wouldn't be a smile. He'd been a spirit for the past twelve years. He knew how things on the other side worked. I only knew how things worked here—at least I thought I did until Kyler showed up.

I slowly turned.

My father stood there looking the same as he had when he was healthy. He never appeared as the frail version of himself, the one I remember from when he passed. And, unfortunately, I was right. He wasn't smiling.

"Hi, Daddy."

"You know I try to stay out of your business," he said. "But I'm worried about you."

"You don't need to worry about me. I'm good. Better than I've been a very long time."

His eyes cast down. He knew I meant since he'd passed. I hadn't meant to make him feel guilty, but it was the truth.

"I'm happy, Daddy," I explained. "Please don't make me feel bad about that."

"You're involved in something you don't understand," he said.

"Do you understand it?"

He shook his head.

"Is there something you know that you're not telling me?"

He shook his head again. "I can see that your feelings for him are growing."

"And what's wrong with that?" I asked.

"I just don't want you to be left with a broken heart," he said.

"I know the risks. And Kyler's worth it. Time spent with him is better than time spent without him," I assured my father.

"I love you, Nora," he said.

"And I love *you*," I said.

"I only want what's best for you."

"Kyler's what's best for me. I feel it in every fiber of my being."

He nodded. "What kind of father would I be if I didn't look out for you?"

"The worst kind," I said with a smile.

He smiled back. "I'll see you soon."

"I know."

He dissipated right there like he always did. I just wished I wasn't left with such a pit in my stomach this time.

* * *

Arriving at the Fletcher's house in a red sweater dress with a platter of Christmas cookies *almost* felt normal. If the guy beside me was visible to everyone but me, it would've been perfect. Mrs. Fletcher opened the door, smiling as soon as she saw me.

"Kyler wanted to spend Christmas Eve with you," I explained. "I hope that's okay."

Her eyes filled with tears. "Oh, my goodness. Of course it's okay." She wrapped her arms around me and held me tightly as I struggled not to drop the cookies. She eventually released me and took the platter from my hands. "Come in. Come in."

I followed her inside with Kyler beside me.

"We were just getting ready to eat." We entered the dining room and I was surprised to see a full spread of food and Mr. Fletcher sitting there alone. He jumped up when he saw me, coming around to hug me. "*Nora.* What a nice surprise," he said as he released me.

"Kyler wanted to spend Christmas Eve with you," I explained.

Mr. Fletcher exchanged a sad look with his wife as she sat down at the table. I could see they were happy I'd come with their son, but having him so close and being unable to see him must've been gut-wrenching.

"Sit," Mr. Fletcher said, gesturing to the other empty seat with the place setting. It broke me to know they'd set a place for Kyler even though he wouldn't be able to join them.

As I sat, I looked to Kyler who slipped into the seat at the other end of the table. His parents looked to that seat too, though they couldn't see him like I could.

"He's sitting in that chair," I explained. "With a content smile on his face."

His mother wept softly, and his father reached over and rubbed a consoling hand over her back.

Most awkward dinner ever.

"Wow. This is a lot of food," I observed, taking in the excessive spread and trying to change the vibe in the room. "Were you expecting more guests?"

Mrs. Fletcher shook her head. "Just a tradition."

"We planned to take the extra food to a homeless shelter," Mr. Fletcher added.

"My mom's the best cook," Kyler said, eying all the food. "I wish I could eat it."

"Kyler said you're the best cook and he wishes he could eat it," I relayed to his mom.

She laughed through her tears. "He was always buttering me up for something."

Kyler laughed and I got the feeling she wasn't lying. He certainly had a way of getting people to do things for him.

"Let's eat," Mr. Fletcher said, likely trying to keep the mood light, as he passed me a huge platter of lasagna. "As you know, this is Ky's favorite."

I looked to Kyler and he smiled. I placed a cheesy square onto my plate. "Looks delicious."

"It is. She adds some secret spice that makes it perfect," Kyler said.

I passed Mrs. Fletcher the lasagna. "He said you add a secret spice."

Laughter burst out of her, full can't-catch-your-breath laughter.

I glanced at Kyler.

"What's so funny?" he asked.

"He wants to know what's so funny," I explained.

Mr. Fletcher joined in on the laughter. "You never told him?" he asked her.

She shook her head through the laughter.

"Told me what?" Kyler asked.

"Told him what?" I asked.

"Mushrooms and onions," she said. "That's the secret spice."

My eyes widened. So did Kyler's. He hated those foods.

"You didn't?" Kyler said aghast.

"He's a bit surprised," I relayed.

Mrs. Fletcher wiped away the tears caused by her laughing. "He wouldn't eat them so I thought if I just stuck them in the food processor and threw them into the sauce, he'd never know. He loved my sauce. So, I could never bear to tell him the truth."

"She's the devil," Kyler said, though I could tell he was amused. "Is she even sorry for deceiving me?"

"He wants to know if you're sorry for deceiving him," I asked.

"Not even a little bit," she admitted which caused us all to break into laughter.

The conversation never ran cold during dinner. They asked Kyler questions, he'd answer, and then I'd relay what he said. They even asked me about me, curious about how I was able to talk with spirits.

"Ask about that detective," Kyler reminded me when we were finishing up.

"Did you speak to the detective yet?" I asked.

They exchanged a look.

"What?" Kyler and I asked at the same time.

"They said there's no indication that anything criminal happened that night," Mr. Fletcher said.

"They claim mist from the river and low temperatures would've contributed to the icy road," Mrs. Fletcher added.

"What about fingerprints on the steering wheel?" Kyler asked.

"Did they fingerprint the car?" I asked.

"There would have been no reason to at the time," Mr. Fletcher said.

"And since then, the car's been totaled," Mrs. Fletcher said. "It's not around even if they wanted to."

"So, they're not going to reopen the investigation?" I asked.

"They said they'll go over everything they have again to see if there's something they missed," Mr. Fletcher said.

"Did you tell them to question Melanie?" I asked.

"They understand our concerns," Mrs. Fletcher said. "And they're planning to follow up on it when she returns from Boston."

"It isn't fair," I said.

"I hate her," Kyler said.

"She'll get what she has coming to her," Mrs. Fletcher said before standing up and gathering some dishes. "Karma always prevails."

"Let me help you," I said as I grabbed some dishes.

Once we finished cleaning, Mrs. Fletcher brewed a pot of coffee. "Will you bring these into the living room?" she asked, handing me my platter of cookies. "They look delicious."

I carried the tray to the living room where the Christmas tree stood. There were only a few gifts beneath the tree.

"Where are all the gifts?" Kyler asked, trailing me into the room.

I knew better than to repeat his question to Mr. Fletcher who sat on the sofa. They were trying to survive while their only child lay in the other room. They really had no reason to celebrate. I placed the cookies down on the coffee table and looked to Mr. Fletcher. "Do you mind if I check out the basement?"

Laughter burst out of Kyler.

"The basement?" Mr. Fletcher asked with furrowed brows.

I shrugged. "I've heard some stories about it."

He chuckled. "I bet you have. Sure. Go ahead."

Kyler led the way to a door in the hallway. "You sure about this?"

"Why wouldn't I be?"

"I don't want you getting all jealous."

I laughed and opened the door, flipping on the light switch before descending the stairs. I stood at the base of the steps impressed by the total man cave surrounding me. My eyes moved from the black leather sectional to the huge wall flat screen to the pool table then the bar. I walked the perimeter of the room looking at all the framed football photos of Kyler filling the walls.

He said nothing as I moved from photo to photo. They spanned his football career, from the time he played in elementary school until he played in college. In some, he caught passes; in others, he was posed with his helmet under his arm.

"I wish you got to see me play," he said.

I spun around to find him leaning against the pool table. "I don't understand it," I admitted.

"I would've explained it to you."

"You still can," I said. "Don't they have games on Christmas?"

He nodded. "I could do that."

I smiled as my eyes drifted around the room. "So, this is where the magic happened."

He tossed back his head and laughed. "Were you hoping to get a little action?"

I shrugged. "What was your signature move?"

"I told you," he said, pushing off the pool table and stalking toward me. "I lit candles and played music."

I slipped my phone from my dress pocket and turned on "Here With Me," the song we'd danced to at the beach. "I just so happen to have the music."

He snaked his arm around my waist and pulled me to him. I giggled as I draped my arms over his shoulders and let him dance us across the basement floor. His green gaze stayed focused on mine, and I would've given anything to know what he was thinking.

"Tuning a tragedy into a comedy," I said.

He nuzzled his nose to mine. "Instead of a comedy could we say a happily ever after?"

I stifled the smile that itched to burst free. "I kind of like that."

"I kind of like *you*," he countered.

I cocked my head. "Kind of?"

He leaned forward and captured my lips. He didn't need to answer that. He was showing me. And, I preferred him showing me any day.

When he eventually pulled away, I rested my head against his shoulder and let him guide me around the space. "Please wake up," I whispered.

"I would if I could."

"Your parents would be so happy to be able to hear your voice and see your smile."

"Just my parents?" he asked.

"I can already hear and see you," I said.

"Is that enough?"

I pulled back so I could meet his eyes. "What?"

"Don't you want to be able to go places with me without people thinking you're speaking to yourself?"

"I don't care what anyone else thinks."

"Don't you want to introduce me to your mom and friends?" he asked.

I said nothing, knowing that could eventually become problematic, but why was he doing this right now?

"I'm falling for you, Nora."

I stilled, my wide eyes locked on his. I'd wanted him to want to be with me. But, now that he put it out in the universe, I was scared that he'd somehow up and disappear.

"I want to give you the world," he continued, "but I know I can't unless I wake up."

"Then wake up," I said again.

He tried to move his mouth into a smile but couldn't manage one. "I don't know how to."

His vulnerability broke me and I just wanted to stay in his arms forever. "Say it again," I said.

"I don't know how to," he repeated.

I shook my head. That wasn't what I meant and he knew it.

He looked me straight in the eyes with his lips pulled up in one corner. "I'm falling for you, Nora."

Fireflies danced in my belly.

"More than I have the right to."

Gahhhhh. He'd be the death of me.

"Nora?" Mr. Fletcher interrupted.

As if caught doing something I shouldn't be, I jumped away from Kyler and dropped my arms. My eyes shifted guiltily to the base of the steps where his parents stood staring at me. "Yeah?" I said, my high-pitched voice reflecting my embarrassment.

Mrs. Fletcher stifled a smile. "What were you doing?" Kyler laughed.

I shot him a look before looking to them. "Dancing."

"*Ohhhh*," Mr. Fletcher said, catching on to what was going on with me and their spirit son.

"Yeah, *oh*," I said, confirming his unspoken assertion.

They exchanged a look and I could see his mom understood as well.

"Why don't you come upstairs so we can give you your gift," Mrs. Fletcher said.

"You got me a gift?" I asked.

"Of course we did. You brought our son back to us," she said.

"You didn't need to get me anything," I assured them. "It makes me happy to be able to bring him home."

Once we were in the living room with coffee and cookies, Mrs. Fletcher handed me a small box with a big red bow on it.

"What did they get you?" Kyler asked from beside me.

I pulled off the bow and then slowly tore open the shiny wrapping paper to reveal a small cardboard box. I opened the cover of the box, but the green tissue paper inside concealed the gift.

"I hope you like it," Mrs. Fletcher said, her eyes on the box.

I reached into the tissue paper until I grasped something solid. I pulled out the most beautiful crystal heart paperweight. As I examined it, all the intricate facets reflected in the lights from the Christmas tree. "It's exquisite."

"I had a feeling our son had already given you his, so I wanted you to have something tangible."

Tears pricked my eyes as I smiled at Kyler.

He shrugged. "What can I say? My mom knows me."

"*You* or your type?" I asked him facetiously.

"Let's just say I know a good thing when I find it." He pressed a kiss to my temple.

I smiled before looking at his mom. "I love it."

She looked pleased with herself.

"Kyler said you know him well," I told her.

"You bringing him here means the world to us," she said.

I didn't say anything because I knew it did. They just didn't realize it meant the world to me too.

* * *

Kyler and I entered my room a short time later. We hadn't spoken about what he'd said but it was all I could think about. He'd fallen for me. Against all odds, we were together. Maybe we could actually work. Maybe it wasn't as crazy as it seemed. I placed his parents' gift on my nightstand beside the photo of me and my parents.

"I'll never be able to give you gifts," he said.

I turned to look at him. "I don't care about gifts."

"Today you don't."

"Oh, we're doing this again?"

"It's just moments like that," his eyes latched onto the heart on my nightstand, "that I remember how not normal we are."

"I don't want normal," I told him. "I've had it and it sucked."

He didn't laugh.

I walked to him and slipped my arms around his hips. "What you said to me at your parents' house. That was a gift."

He cocked his head. "Liar."

"Spirit."

"I'm serious, Nora."

"Stopping killing the mood," I said.

His lips twitched. "I didn't realize there was a mood."

"Oh, there's a mood," I assured him.

He laughed. "Well then, I'm starting to think there *is* something I can give you."

"See? I knew you were more creative than that," I said.

He lifted me off my feet and carried me to the bed, laying me down but stepping back. He pulled off his hoodie and T-shirt in one smooth motion.

I pushed myself onto my elbows, enjoying the show. "Keep going," I urged.

He shook his head with a devious glint in his eyes as he walked to the foot of the bed. He reached down and removed my ankle boots. He moved to the hem of my dress and tugged it up to my bra. He stared down at my red thong before eyeing my legs and sending a shiver scampering up them. He pushed my legs apart and crawled between them.

"Oh," I gasped, realizing his intent.

"Merry Christmas," he said before moving his mouth between my thighs.

CHAPTER 20

"Merry Christmas," Kyler whispered as I shifted slightly in his arms, my cheek pressed to his bare chest.

"Merry Christmas," I said with my eyes still closed. "Did Santa come?"

"I don't know. Were you a good girl this year?" he asked.

"Define good?"

He chuckled before pressing a kiss to the top of my head. "Your phone's been blowing up all morning."

"Probably just my mom wishing me a Merry Christmas before she gets here." I opened my eyes and moved my head so I could see him.

He leaned down and pressed his lips to mine. "Can't wait to meet her," he said.

"Did I say you were meeting her?"

"No, but I expected her to want to meet me."

I smiled. "Oh, she wants to meet you alright."

"Can she see spirits too?"

I shook my head.

"But you said people could if they wanted to," he said.

"She tried to see my dad, but no matter what I had her do, she just couldn't see him. I thought she might've been too scared."

"Scared?"

"Yeah, like it would be too hard to see him again and then not be able to see him. Like, if he was gone, she could come to terms with that eventually. But if he popped in when he felt like it, it would just make it harder to move on."

"Makes sense."

"I kind of think me being able to see him and her not was the catalyst for her to start being a traveling nurse. That way, she didn't have to live here without him."

Kyler's eyes conveyed sadness, and I wondered if he was thinking about my mom and dad, or if his thoughts were on our own fate.

I grabbed my phone off the nightstand and checked it. Five texts from an unknown number filled the screen.

7:02 It's Daci. I'm using my brother's phone. I need you to do me a huge favor…

7:06 The café's alarm keeps going off. I think it's malfunctioning.

7:10 Nora are you there?

7:12 Could you pleeeeassse go punch in the code and turn it off.

7:15 I really don't want to leave my family.

"Shit." I checked the time. 7:20.

"What?" Kyler asked.

"Daci needs me to go turn off the alarm at the café."

"Right now?"

"She's at her parents' almost an hour away." I sent her back a text that I could and rolled out of bed. "I'll be back in ten minutes."

"I'll come with you," he said, starting to get up.

"Oh, no you don't. I want you right here when I get back. I wasn't ready to get up yet."

"How can I argue when it's one of the only gifts I can give you today?"

"Smart boy." I grabbed a sweatshirt from my drawer and pulled it over my tank top.

"Did you just call me a boy?" he asked, rolling onto his side with his cheek in his palm.

I laughed as I pulled on yoga pants.

"Because I'm pretty damn sure I'm all man."

I rolled my eyes. "Be right back." I headed toward the door.

"Hey," Kyler called.

I stopped, glancing back at him in my bed wishing I was still right beside him.

"Best Christmas ever."

I laughed and turned back to the door.

"Wait!"

I stopped again and turned around. "What? I've gotta go."

He stared at me long and hard like he had something really important to say. "Never mind."

I released a sigh, wishing I knew what he wanted to say. But, if I wanted to be back to him in ten minutes, I needed to go. I hurried downstairs, grabbed my coat, and headed outside still pushing my arms into the sleeves. Izzy's car was parked behind mine. I hadn't even heard her come in last night.

I took off toward the café. Silence surrounded me. I felt like George Bailey hurrying down a deserted street when everyone else was inside with loved ones—opening gifts or still sound asleep in bed. I turned the corner onto the main road. I expected to see someone taking an early morning stroll, but the sidewalks were vacant, the shops were dark, and it was eerily quiet.

I neared the café, cutting down the alley between it and the gift shop next door. The moment I turned the corner to the back lot, an explosion of pain tore through my chest as a solid object slammed into me, stealing away my breath. I fell back, landing on my ass on the hard pavement as I clutched my chest. Something was wrong. I couldn't catch my breath. My heart raced. My vision blurred before I was swallowed up by a cloud of nothingness.

Kyler

Where the hell was Nora? I checked the alarm clock on her nightstand for the hundredth time. It had been thirty minutes. Nothing should have taken that long.

I knew I should've gone with her, but the way she wanted me in bed when she got back did weird things to my brain. I climbed out from under the covers and yanked on my clothes. I rushed outside and jogged toward the café. If I had a cell phone, I could have just called her. All that normal stuff just wasn't ever going to be us.

I turned onto the main street, surprised to find it so deserted. I hurried over to the front door of the café and shielded my eyes from the sun, staring inside. Lights were off, no one was inside, and no alarm was ringing. I spun away from the door and moved through the alley, rounding the building to the back parking lot.

I froze as fear grabbed hold of my body.

Nora was sprawled on the ground, her arms and legs contorted in unnatural positions and her eyes closed. *Fuuuuck.* I rushed over, dropping to my knees at her side and shaking her. "Nora. Wake up! What's wrong? Tell me what's wrong." Her eyes didn't open. I looked over her but couldn't see any blood—or anything else signifying what was wrong. I dropped my ear to her chest and listened. I could only barely hear a heartbeat.

I sat up and looked around the deserted area. "Help!" I screamed. "Help me!" My body trembled as I scooped her up and rocked her. "Wake up, baby. Please, wake up." Tears glazed my eyes. No one could hear me. No one was going to find her. No one was going to save her.

Think. *Fucking* think!

I lay Nora back down. "I'll be right back," I assured her before running out into the middle of the street. I looked from side to side. No one walked around. No cars drove on the road. I ran down the street looking every which way. I looked back at the café and closed my eyes.

I was fucking helpless.

Unless…

I ran back to Nora's house, bounding up the stairs. The water in the shower ran. Izzy was awake! I tried the knob but my hand went right through it. Desperate times. I slipped through the locked door and slammed my hand into the shower curtain causing the rod to almost come off the wall.

Izzy screamed and yanked open the curtain, using the rest of it to cover her body. "Nora?" Her head whipped around. I knew she couldn't see me. But she had to know I was there. I noticed the fogged mirror and rushed to it. Using my finger, I wrote *Nora.*

"Oh my God," Izzy screeched, watching as the letters materialized before her eyes.

I continued writing. *Is hurt behind café. Call 911.*

"Shit!" Izzy wrapped herself in a towel and grabbed her phone from the sink. I didn't wait. I raced back to the café with one thought in mind. Get Nora to the hospital.

I ran through the alley and dropped to the ground beside her right where I'd left her, lowering my ear to her chest again and listening for her heartbeat. It was faint. So damn faint. "Hurry up!" I screamed to the ambulance that couldn't hear me. I kissed her forehead. "Stay with me. *Please* stay with me." I lifted her into my arms so her head didn't touch the pavement. "I'm here, Nora. I'm right here. Help's coming." As soon as I said it, sirens sounded in the distance. "Do you hear that? They're coming for you. They're gonna get you the help you need." I looked around. What the hell happened to her?

The sirens neared and flashing red lights illuminated the alley.

"Nora?!" Izzy called, running out of the alley and into the lot. "Jesus Christ!" she screamed upon seeing her. "The ambulance is here, Kyler. You're gonna have to lay her down so they aren't seeing her levitating like I am right now."

I lay her down as Izzy dropped beside her. "Nora? What the hell happened? Wake up, honey." Her eyes moved over her body before her ear dropped to her chest and her hand found her wrist, checking her vitals. "Help is here. They're gonna get you whatever you need."

There was the sound of footsteps and then two EMTs rounded the building with a stretcher.

"What happened?" they asked Izzy.

"I don't know. I just found her like this. I'm a nurse. She has bradycardia. You need to get her on an IV to increase her blood pressure."

One EMT felt for a pulse. "She's right," he said to his partner. "She's fading."

"What's that mean she's fading?" I demanded, though I knew no one could hear me.

The other EMT knelt beside her, checking her neck. "No sign of asphyxiation," he said.

His partner spoke into a walkie attached to his shoulder. "One female. Unresponsive. Send police. Could be an attack."

An attack? Jesus Christ. Jesus fucking Christ.

"Nora, please wake up," Izzy begged.

"Okay, you're going to need to back up," one of the EMTs said to Izzy. "We've got to transport her to the hospital."

Izzy moved back, crossing her arms and crying as they positioned themselves at Nora's feet and head before counting down and lifting her onto the stretcher.

"Are you coming in the ambulance?" one of the EMTs asked her.

"Yes," Izzy and I answered.

They wheeled the stretcher through the alley to the ambulance out front. They pulled open the back door and slid the stretcher in before one of them climbed inside allowing Izzy (and me) in with them. The other closed us inside and hurried around to the driver's seat.

We pulled away with a lurch and the siren sounded. Within minutes, the EMT had Nora hooked up to oxygen, an IV, and was monitoring her heartbeat. Izzy kept Nora's hand clasped in hers, her finger from her other hand monitoring her pulse even though the monitor showed her slowed pulse on the screen.

I crouched at Nora's other side, just needing to touch her. "You're gonna be okay," I said, having no idea if that was even the truth. "You've got this." After everything she'd done for me, everything we'd been through, how could she not be okay? I was supposed to go first. Hell, I was halfway there.

"Come on, Nora," Izzy whispered. "You need to be okay. *I* need you. And, Kyler needs you."

I glanced up, not expecting her to mention me.

"He helped me find you," she said. "If he hadn't, who knows what…" she began to sob.

"You need to be strong for your friend," the EMT said.

Izzy pushed away her tears and nodded.

The ambulance lurched, and we stopped. I whirled around, realizing we'd arrived at the hospital.

The other EMT pulled open the back door. "You can get out," he said to Izzy who climbed out.

I waited until they pulled Nora's stretcher out and then climbed out, following alongside as a group of doctors met us at the sliding doors, getting information from the EMTs.

"Please wait in the waiting area," one of the doctors said to Izzy. "We'll keep you informed."

"Stay with her, Kyler," Izzy said, though no one but me paid any attention to her words.

I ran alongside the stretcher as they rushed Nora through the busy emergency room and into a less crowded hallway in the back. The doctors began shouting orders to the nurses. "When we get in there, start a—"

My head whipped around as a stretcher rushed past us in the opposite direction. My parents were hunched over the side of the stretcher. "Mom?"

CHAPTER 21

Kyler

My mother looked up just in time to see Nora in the stretcher going in the opposite direction. "Nora?" My mother looked confused, but her attention was pulled back to the doctor running alongside my stretcher.

I knew the doctors were going to help Nora, so I followed after my parents. I needed to know what the hell was happening. Why was I there? What had happened? And, was Nora's condition connected to mine?

A doctor and two nurses met my parents and the EMTs who'd been pushing the stretcher.

"His intracranial pressure readings became erratic," the EMT explained to the doctor.

"How about his heart rate, blood pressure, and breathing?" the doctor asked.

"All normal," he explained while my mother fought to keep her composure.

"We're going to have to alleviate the pressure," the doctor said. "He's a strong young man. He can pull through this."

A nurse placed her hand on my mother's arm. "We've got it from here. You can wait in the waiting room. We'll keep you informed as soon as we know anything."

With that, they wheeled me into the operating room, leaving my frightened parents standing outside.

My father wrapped his arms around my mother. "He's going to be okay," he assured her, though there was little conviction in his words.

"He hasn't been okay in over a year," she said as she buried her head in his shoulder and sobbed.

"I'm right here," I said. "I can hear you. I'm gonna pull through this."

"Oh my God," my mother said, pulling away from my father.

"What?" he asked.

"Nora," she said as if she'd forgotten. "I saw them wheeling her in."

"What?" he asked.

My mom took off down the hallway, her head whipping from side to side searching the rooms for Nora. But her pursuit was futile given all the doors were marked *Authorized Personnel Only*. She eventually stepped into the waiting room. She searched the area. Izzy sat in the corner with her face in her hands. "Nora's friend Izzy is right there," I said, hoping beyond hope my mother could hear me.

My mother walked over to an older woman seated in the opposite corner of the waiting room from Izzy. "Are you here with Nora?" my mother asked the woman.

The woman shook her head.

My mother looked around, spotting an older couple along the side wall of the room, closer to Izzy. She approached them. "Are you here with Nora?"

They shook their heads.

Izzy dropped her hands and looked to my mother. "Did you ask about Nora?"

My mom rushed over to her. "Yes. Do you know her?"

"She's my roommate," Izzy said.

My dad hurried into the waiting room, likely just locating my mother who'd taken off like a bat out of hell.

"What happened to her?" my mom asked Izzy.

"I don't know," Izzy said. "I found her outside the cafe where she works," Izzy explained. "There was no blood or anything, but her pulse was almost nonexistent."

My mother clasped her mouth with her hand. "Oh my God."

"How do you know Nora?"

My parents exchanged a look that told me they didn't know how to explain.

"She knows our son Kyler," my father said.

Izzy's eyes widened. "Kyler's the one who helped me find her."

"You can see him too?" my father asked.

She shook her head with tears glazing her eyes. "No. But he wrote on my foggy mirror."

My mom exhaled a deep sigh through her tears.

"Is that how you knew to come here?" Izzy asked them.

"No. Ky's here too," my father explained. "His intracranial pressure readings were erratic this morning. The doctor's relieving the pressure right now."

"This morning?" Izzy asked.

They nodded.

"So, around the same time as whatever happened to Nora?"

"You think it's related?" my mother asked.

Izzy shrugged. "I have no idea."

I left the three of them and searched for my other self. I found me in the operating room, but once I passed through the door, I couldn't get within five feet of the operating table. "Wake up," I willed myself. "Nora needs you."

The doctors spoke in low voices as they worked to drain the fluid from my brain. I spun away from them, but a bout of dizziness washed over me. I steadied myself before heading back into the hallway and searching for Nora's room. Once I found it, two doctors—a male and female—stood over her, while two nurses stood nearby. The doctors' voices were fading in and out as if I was in some kind of dream. I wondered if the pressure in my other brain was affecting this brain.

"...aortic aneurysm," the male doctor said.

I placed my hand on Nora's. "I'm here, Nora."

"...CT scan," the female doctor said.

I squeezed Nora's hand. "I'm not going anywhere."

"...internal bleeding," the female doctor said.

I stared at the oxygen tubes attached to her nose. "I never got to tell you all the things I wanted to tell you. So, I think you just need to wake up so I can."

"...blunt force trauma," the male doctor noted.

"What happened, sweet girl?" Tears glazed my eyes. "You promised you'd be back in ten minutes."

"She could die if it ruptures," the female doctor said.

My head shot up. Die?

"Let's get the CT scan," the male doctor said.

"Then decide," the female doctor added.

"Go talk to her family," the male doctor said. "I'll get her prepped."

I followed the doctor out of the operating room. She removed her gloves and mask and discarded them before making her way to the waiting room.

Once we entered the small space, I spotted my parents. I looked to Izzy who sat beside a woman who I recognized from the photo in Nora's room. And though she looked older, there was no doubt it was Nora's mom. Same dark hair. Same dusting of freckles on her nose.

The doctor approached them. "Nora's family?" she asked.

They jumped to their feet. "Yes," they said in unison.

"How is she?" Nora's mother asked, her voice so similar to Nora's.

"She suffered blunt force trauma to the chest," the doctor explained. "So, we're checking to see if she suffered an aortic aneurysm."

Both of them gasped, indicating the diagnosis wasn't good.

"We're getting her in for a CT scan right now," the doctor said.

"Do you think it ruptured?" Nora's mother asked.

"That's why we're scanning her," the doctor explained.

At the same time, another doctor approached my parents. I spun to hear what was being said as they spoke to them. "…exhausted our options," the doctor said as I moved closer.

"We can't stop the building intracranial pressure," he said. "He will be brain-dead by morning."

A guttural sob tore out of my mother as her knees gave out and my father caught her.

"There are no other options?" my father asked as he held my mother.

The room began to spin around me. Weightlessness took hold of me. The building intracranial pressure was catching up with this version of me. I tried to hold on. I tried to hear what my doctor was saying. What Nora's doctor was saying. But darkness swallowed me whole.

CHAPTER 22

Nora

"Nora?" Izzy's voice faintly played in my mind. But why was she at the café? I needed to get back to Kyler. The sight of him in my bed, knowing he was waiting for me to return, was such a gift. "Nora, honey. You've got to wake up."

I attempted to open my eyes, but the unexpected weight of my eyelids prohibited it. I tried to speak, but my mouth was so dry I couldn't get my tongue and lips to cooperate. What had happened? I had faint recollections of an explosion of pain like I'd never endured before. Then nothing.

"Nora?" It was my mother's voice.

Why was she at the café?

"It's time to wake up," my father said.

Okay, this was getting weird. Why were they all here?

"Has she woken up?" an unfamiliar man asked.

"Not yet," my mother said.

"Well, keep talking to her. It shouldn't be long now," he assured them.

Long for what?

"Don't forget," he continued. "When she comes to, don't bombard her with too much information. There's plenty of time to get information from her and give information to her."

What does that mean? What information do I have? And what information do they have?

Sleep pulled me back under and there was nothing I could do to stop it.

* * *

"Nora?" a woman said. "Are you awake?"

My eyes cracked, but the light was too bright and they quickly snapped shut. I wanted to ask where I was, but my cotton mouth prevented me from speaking.

"You've had a lot of visitors wanting to see you," she continued. "So many people love you."

Her voice echoed as if distant, but I knew she was nearby. I tried to turn my head, but it was a weight that I couldn't quite lift.

"Oh, honey. Don't try to move," she said. "I'll go get the doctor."

I had no clue if the doctor ever arrived because sleep pulled me back under, and I didn't even try to fight it.

* * *

I opened my eyes, an easier feat now that darkness surrounded me. My eyes shifted slowly around me. I was in a hospital room. I was in a bed attached to wires and tubes. Machines beeped around me. "Hello?" I whispered since it was all I could manage.

No one responded.

"Kyler?" I tried again.

Silence.

"Are you here?" I asked.

Silence.

For the first time since he walked into the café, I couldn't feel his presence. Something was wrong. Something was terribly wrong.

My heart monitor accelerated, mirroring the pounding in my chest.

A nurse burst into the room, bringing a gust of air and blinding light from the hallway that caused my eyes to squeeze nearly shut. "Nora?"

"Why am I here?" I asked.

"You need to calm down," she said. "Your heart rate is accelerated." She pushed something into the IV that I now realized was in the back of my hand. The heart monitor slowed along with my racing heart. "You've been through a lot. You need to keep your heart rate normal. We don't want you to overexert yourself."

"Where's my mom?" I asked.

"It's three in the morning," she informed me. "I'm sure she'll be back in the morning like she has been every day this week."

"Week?" I croaked.

"Get some rest. We'll explain everything in the morning," she said, before walking out of my room and closing me in the darkness once again.

I turned my head to the side where I saw my phone and a cup of water on the nearby table. Using all the strength I could gather, I reached over and slipped my phone off the table. A pain throbbed in the center of my chest. I pressed my other hand over the spot, feeling a bandage beneath my hospital gown. I pointed my phone at my face and it powered on, lighting up the dark room and causing me to squint.

Texts from Izzy, Daci, Rick, and Zoe filled my screen. All asking how I was. All asking me to call when I felt up to it.

What the hell had happened?

And where was Kyler?

CHAPTER 23

"You're awake," a doctor said as he swept into my hospital room the next morning. "How are you feeling?"

"I have no idea. Why am I here?" I said.

"First things first," he said, leaning over me and pressing his stethoscope to my chest. "I need to check on your new heart."

"New heart?" I gasped.

"Relax, Nora. We wouldn't want you overworking it."

Tears stung my eyes. "Why did I need a new heart?"

"You suffered an aortic aneurysm."

"*What?*"

"You were in some type of accident that caused blunt force trauma to your chest."

"An accident?"

"You don't remember?" he asked.

I shook my head.

"That trauma caused an aneurysm which is a balloon-like bulge in your aorta," he explained. "It ruptured causing bleeding inside your body. Since that can be fatal, we needed to act fast. We hadn't considered a transplant, but there was one in close proximity with the same blood type as yours."

My mind reeled. Aneurysm? Heart transplant? Accident?

"You'll make a full recovery and be able to do everything you could do before."

I tried to nod my understanding, but the gravity of the information overwhelmed me, immobilizing me. My eyes moved around the room hoping Kyler was nearby, but all I found were flowers and balloons. "How long will I be in here?"

"Oh, I think you're looking at another week. Get some rest. You need to stay strong for that heart."

I didn't know how to reply; everything felt like I was in a dream.

"Do you have any other questions for me?" he asked.

Only a hundred. But I needed time to wrap my head around everything before I could even begin to ask questions *and* retain his answers. "I don't think so."

He patted my arm before walking toward the door. "Happy New Year," he said before disappearing in the hallway.

New Year?

I closed my eyes and dragged in a deep breath. A week had passed and I had no recollection of it. None of it seemed real. *Was* I dreaming?

* * *

The sound of footsteps woke me from a sound sleep. But why was my room dark again? Had I slept all day? Had I missed my mom's visit?

A police officer entered my hospital room. "Nora?"

I nodded.

"I'm Officer Kent. I've been assigned to your case," he explained, moving to the side of my bed. He crossed his arms and stared down at me. "How much do you remember about Christmas morning?"

I thought back as best as I could. To how happy I'd been to wake up in Kyler's arms. To Daci's texts about the alarm. "My boss needed me to check the café. I ran over and then…then I had an accident," I said, repeating the doctor's words.

"What type of accident?"

I struggled to remember what occurred once I turned the corner to the back parking lot. The explosion of pain. The inability to catch my breath. Landing on my ass. "I think someone hit me."

"Someone?" he asked, opening up his small notepad and preparing to take notes with his pen.

I racked my brain for anything else that could help, but it was as if I'd dreamed it and the memory was slowly fleeting, never to be remembered again. Frustration grabbed hold of me. This was how Kyler must've felt about his accident. The information was so close, yet it was so far away.

And, where was Kyler? Where was everyone I knew and loved?

"Is there anyone who would want to hurt you?" Officer Kent asked.

My eyes shifted to his. Only one person would want to hurt me. "Melanie."

"Melanie who?"

Could she really have done this to me? Could she really have caused both my and Kyler's accidents? This was all too much. "Is this a dream?" I asked Officer Kent.

"A dream?"

My eyes shot around the room. "Like, am I really in the hospital? Did I really have a heart transplant?"

"I'm afraid this isn't a dream," he said with disappointment in his eyes. "But, I can see that I need to give you some more time."

"That would probably be a good idea," I said, grateful that he sensed my frustration.

"Would you mind if I stopped by when you're feeling better to talk about this some more?" he asked.

"Of course," I said.

"Get some rest," he offered before walking toward the door.

"Officer?"

He glanced back at me.

"Talk to my boss, Daci. There are cameras at the café that might be able to help."

He nodded his appreciation and turned to walk away.

"Officer?" I called again.

He turned back around.

"Is there anyone waiting to see me?" I asked, knowing it sounded feeble.

"It's kind of late. I've been here for two hours waiting for you to wake up. But, if anyone's waiting, I'll send them in," he assured me before disappearing into the hallway.

I closed my eyes and tried to replay Christmas morning over in my mind. Kyler in my bed felt so good. So right. He was going to "meet" my mom. Then Daci's texts. I only planned to be a few minutes. He told me he'd come with me, but I told him to wait for me. Then everything imploded. Could Melanie really be the cause of me being here?

"Nora?"

I opened my eyes and found Mrs. Fletcher in my doorway. "Hi."

"May I?" she asked, tentatively stepping inside.

"Of course." I motioned to the chair beside my bed.

"It's so nice to see you awake," she said, lowering herself slowly into the chair.

"I've been asleep for a while, haven't I?"

She nodded, though her eyes hid something I couldn't quite read. "No one could see you while you were in the ICU."

"I was in there for a while?"

She nodded, and it was then that I noticed her bloodshot eyes. "Mrs. Fletcher? What's going on?"

"You and Kyler came to the hospital at the same time," she explained.

"What? Is he okay?"

"His intracranial pressure spiked," she explained, her voice low and pained.

"Is it better now?" I asked. "Did they fix it?"

She shook her head.

Tears blurred my vision.

"We had to take him off the ventilator."

Nausea climbed up my throat as my head swam. "What?"

She nodded as tears trailed down her cheeks.

I closed my eyes and tears streamed out of them. "I should have been there with him."

"It happened so fast," she said.

"He must've been so scared," I said, finally looking at her.

"I wasn't supposed to tell you yet," she said, covering my hand with her own. "But I knew you needed to know."

"I'm so sorry," I said, knowing the sentiment was inadequate.

"I'm so sorry for you too," she said. "I know Ky loved you."

Even though he'd never said it, I knew he did too. Now, I'd never get the chance to hear it from his own lips. I'd never feel his arms wrapped around me. I'd never experience him laughing at something I said. I'd never get to experience what being loved by him felt like again. "I loved him too."

"He hasn't visited you?" she asked, a sliver of hope in her voice.

I shook my head. "I knew something didn't feel right."

"I hope it's not your heart," she said with a hopeful look despite her bloodshot eyes.

"You heard?" I asked.

"It's Ky's heart."

I blinked hard. "What?"

"The transplant. It's his heart you have inside of you," she said.

I pressed my hand to my chest—right over my heart. The rhythmic beat throbbed beneath the bandage under my hospital gown as tears rushed out of my eyes. "How?"

"It was his brain that was failing, not his heart," she said through her own tears.

"Oh my God," I said, unable to believe what she was telling me. "This isn't right."

"Oh, sweetie. It's exactly what he would've wanted," she assured me.

I reached for her hand. She let me take it, standing as I guided it to my chest, right over Kyler's heart. "Do you feel him?"

She closed her eyes and nodded, silently weeping as his heart beat beneath her hand.

"I'll take good care of it," I assured her.

She looked me in the eyes. "I have no doubt about that." She eventually removed her hand and sat back in the seat. "Thank you for that. I think I really needed it."

"I'm here for you. Any time," I assured her.

"Thank you…but I was hoping you might be able to do one other thing for me," she said.

"Anything."

"Will you speak at Ky's services?" she asked.

"I didn't miss them?"

"We already had a private burial, but we're holding off on the services until you can be there," she said. "Do you think you'll be up to speaking?"

I choked on a sob. "I'd be honored."

She nodded before standing up. "I think I might have overstayed my welcome," she said. "Not to mention broken the rules by telling you the truth."

"Your son was good about telling me the truth, so I wouldn't expect anything less from his mother," I said, trying to smile through my grief.

Once she left the room, I cried for a long time. I hadn't felt that alone since meeting Kyler. He'd come into my life like a whirlwind and taught me so much about the person I was and the person I deserved to be loved by. Now he was gone, and even though I had a new heart—*his* heart—it felt completely and utterly broken. I didn't know if I'd ever recover from that kind of pain.

Maybe I never would.

CHAPTER 24

"Take it easy," Izzy said as she helped me through our front door.

"I'm fine," I assured her.

"Well, your mom will kick my ass if I don't watch your every move like I promised."

Izzy had taken a leave of absence to stay with me through my recovery. And, my mom had taken a closer assignment so she could stay with us on the weekends.

I looked around our empty living room. My eyes were pulled to Kyler's sofa. I envisioned him lying there, unable to sleep.

"I'm gonna go grab your stuff from the car," Izzy said. "Do you need anything?"

I shook my head.

"I want you to sit down. Gather your strength for the flight of steps upstairs."

Once she disappeared outside, I took in the empty room. The silence. I hadn't realized how much space Kyler had taken up. His smile. His laugh. His gazes. I moved to the sofa and slowly lowered myself down, careful not to irritate my incision as I did. The bottle of cologne I'd bought sat on the table. I reached for it and lifted it to my nose. Tears pricked my eyes as the smell of it brought upon a barrage of memories. And, as hard as it was to let those memories in, I needed to feel close to him. I needed to feel like my whole world hadn't collapsed. I placed the bottle back on the table and lay down.

I covered my face with my hands and sobbed. Life was so unfair. A girl who'd killed Kyler *and* attacked me got to live. Why not Kyler?

Though there may never be proof of what Melanie had done in Kyler's car, she was currently in prison on aggravated assault charges thanks to the cameras on the gift shop next to the café. She *had* been the one who attacked me with a wooden board Christmas morning. It's why she pled guilty and received ten years as opposed to the maximum thirty she could've been facing by fighting it in court.

I hated Melanie.

I hated her for what she'd done to him.

I hated her for what she'd done to me.

I hated her for what she'd done to *us*.

"Nora?"

I lowered my hands and looked to Izzy standing in the doorway with her arms filled with flowers and a bunch of get-well balloons in her hand.

"Oh, honey," she said, noting my tear-stained cheeks. "Just tell me what you need and I'll do it." She released the balloons so they scattered all over our ceiling and placed the flowers down on the table. She moved to me and sat on the edge of the sofa.

I shook my head as tears continued to fall. "It's not fair."

"It's not," she agreed. "There's nothing fair about it."

"I loved him," I said.

She rubbed a soothing hand over my forehead. "I know. And he loved you."

I nodded. "He did. He really did." She wiped away some of the tears on my cheeks, and I wished the gesture brought me more comfort than it did. I was numb. Numb because he was gone. Numb because I had his heart. Numb because it shouldn't have ended this way. "We danced under the stars." I sniffled. "Did I tell you that?"

"You didn't," she said sharing a sad smile. "That sounds romantic."

"It was."

A long silence passed and I appreciated her not trying to fill it with words of wisdom that I really didn't want to hear.

"I slept with him," I admitted.

"Is that even possible?"

"Oh, it was possible."

"How was it?" she asked, like the nosy friend she was.

"Amazing," I said.

"I'm glad you waited for the right guy. Because he *was* the right guy, Nora," she assured me. "Just because he's not here anymore doesn't change that."

I sighed, knowing she was right despite it hurting so damn much.

"You have incredible memories with him," she said.

And though I knew she meant it to be reassuring, it only left more of a hollow in my chest. "Why did this have to happen, Iz?"

"Because life's a crazy journey." She lay down beside me and wrapped her arms around me like a parent comforting their child. I relaxed into her, needing her strength—needing her comfort. "You just never know when it's gonna throw you a curveball like this. That's the risk of getting to live this life. The wonderful days are balanced by the tragic ones."

"That's depressing," I said.

She laughed. "It is."

"I'm not gonna be okay," I admitted.

"I know it doesn't seem like it now, but you will be," she assured me. "You're a survivor, Nora. You're the strongest person I know."

"Liar," I muttered.

"I'm not. Why do you think all these spirits come to you?"

"Because I'm a sucker and will help them and put their needs before my own?"

"Because you're compassionate and brave and a hell of a human being."

"You have to say that," I said.

"No, I don't. You of all people should know I can be a real bitch sometimes."

I wanted to laugh, but it just wouldn't come. I closed my eyes and tried not to envision Kyler in my mind. Tried not to picture my final moments with him. And, though I tried to stop the sadness from flooding my brain, it was as if my memories played on a constant loop and they wouldn't stop. "Why didn't I let him come to the café with me?"

"Don't do this, Nora."

"He wanted to come with me. Why couldn't I just let him?"

"Because you couldn't have known Melanie was pretending to be Daci," Izzy assured me.

"But if I just—"

"I love you, but I'm not gonna let you blame yourself. He couldn't have stopped her even if he was there."

I didn't respond. She may have been right. Melanie's attack came out of nowhere.

"It's gonna take time," Izzy said. "And, I promise you, I'll be by your side every step of the way."

* * *

I lay on the sofa with a blanket over my lap as the fire crackled in the fireplace. I'd eaten half a jar of peanut butter with a spoon. Izzy had just helped me shower and rebandage my incision.

She laughed from her spot on the loveseat. "Oh, my God. This is even funnier than I remember," she said as *The Hangover* streamed on our television.

"It's such a guy movie," I mumbled.

She continued laughing at the craziness on the screen, and I wished I could laugh too.

When she asked what movie we should watch, I suggested Kyler's favorite, thinking it would make me feel closer to him. But all it had done was make me wonder what parts made him laugh the hardest. Which character he liked the best. Which situations he found the most outrageous.

"How's that peanut butter?" she asked, confused by my new choice of snack.

"Delicious," I said, eating a spoonful.

She laughed before she turned back to the television. "Come on, Nora. How can you not laugh at that?" She thrust her hand out at the television as her laughter grew louder.

Wasn't it obvious?

"What movie's next?" she asked.

"I was thinking *Old School*. I love the streaking scene," I said.

"I'm in."

"Maybe tomorrow night we could go in the backyard, and I could show you some of the constellations Kyler showed me."

She cocked her head, not even bothering to disguise the sympathy in her eyes. "Will it help?"

I shrugged.

"Constellations it is!" she declared before laughing at the movie again.

CHAPTER 25

My black heels echoed up the steps behind the pulpit. I stood tall and looked out over the entire church. Not a pew was empty. The Fletchers sat in the front pew beside his living grandmother. The one I'd seen at the bridge sat beside her. Bono sat in the second row with a bunch of guys I assumed were Kyler's high school friends. My mom, Izzy, and Daci sat in the middle of the church all nodding reassuringly at me. I took that as my cue to begin.

"I know most of you don't know me," I began, needing no notes since I was speaking from the heart. "But I'm the girl who was lucky enough to get Kyler's heart. Now I know what you're thinking. He was this gorgeous charismatic guy who got lots of attention and there was a long list of girls who got his heart over the years…"

People laughed and it made me happy to know my joke was helping to alleviate the somber mood in the church.

"Well, I'll have you know," I continued, placing my hand over my heart and feeling the small bandage beneath my dress. "I literally have his heart. It's the most amazing gift he could've ever given me. And, without it, I wouldn't be standing here today. Kyler saved my life that day, but he'd actually saved me before that by loving me. He showed me that I didn't need to be afraid of taking risks. He showed me that not every guy can't be trusted. He showed me what real love feels like even if it only lasts for a short time."

Tears trailed down Mrs. Fletcher's cheeks. Her courage through all of this urged me on.

"Whether you visited Kyler lately or you hadn't seen him since before the accident, I know he loved all of you. He understood it was difficult to see him the way he'd been this last year. But he never once thought you didn't love and care about him." I met the teary eyes of people in the church. "So, I guess the Fletchers wanted me to speak today because a piece of Kyler will always be alive in me, and for that, I am eternally grateful." My eyes moved back to theirs. "I will never take the responsibility of carrying his heart for granted. I will treat his heart like the precious gift it is." I glanced up and spoke to the heavens. "I love you, Kyler Fletcher. You are the best thing that ever happened to me." I moved away from the pulpit with tears in my eyes. I made my way across the altar, past the huge floral arrangements, and by the gold framed photo of Kyler that sat on a stand at the front of the alter.

Mr. Fletcher stood from the front pew and stepped into the aisle, taking me by the arm and assisting me back to the seat beside him and Mrs. Fletcher. She took my hand as soon as I sat, holding it tightly as Kyler's friends stepped up to the pulpit and told funny stories about him for the next hour. I could imagine Kyler watching from beyond and laughing.

The Fletchers and I were the last ones in the church, getting to spend the final minutes with "him." I slipped a white rose out of the biggest arrangement, lifting it to my nose and smelling it.

"Are you ready?" Mrs. Fletcher asked.

I shook my head. "I just need a few more minutes. Izzy will bring me over."

"Take all the time you need," she said before hugging me. Tears filled my eyes and I knew it would be some time before I could look at the Fletchers without crying. She released me and Mr. Fletcher hugged me. "We'll see you in a bit." He stepped away and took his wife's hand. They made their way down the aisle and out of the church, leaving me alone.

I dropped down into the front pew and released a long breath. This wasn't how it was supposed to end. There was supposed to be a happy ending for the two of us. We weren't supposed to be the tragedy.

"Nora?"

I glanced over my shoulder.

My mom stood by the church door. "You coming?"

I shook my head. "I can't leave yet. I'll meet you at the Fletcher's."

"You sure?" she asked and I could tell she didn't know if she should leave me.

I nodded. I couldn't leave him just yet. I watched until she disappeared outside, then I turned back to Kyler's photo. He seemed to be looking directly at me. My tears fell freely because I knew the moment I walked out of that church, Kyler would only be a memory. I didn't even have a photo of the two of us to look at when I needed a reminder of our time together.

I heard the sound of her high heels clicking down the aisle, before Izzy sat down beside me. "How long do you plan on staying here?" she asked, her voice gentle.

"Forever."

She wrapped her arm around my shoulder and pulled me gently into her. "You can't stay here forever. Kyler wouldn't want that. He wanted you to go out there and live your life."

She was right. He would've hated me putting my life on hold for him. But how could I go on living like he hadn't come into my life and made it better? How could I ever even think about moving on after I had perfection?

"I'm gonna say goodbye," I whispered, slipping out from Izzy's arm and standing.

She stayed seated as I stepped up to Kyler's photo. I traced my finger along its gaudy gold frame. "You changed my life, Kyler Fletcher. It's gonna take time for me to heal because I fell for you too. Every part of you. In such a short time, you gave me so many beautiful memories. That's the hard part. Nothing and no one will ever compare. How could they? But I'll make you this promise. I'll go out and live my life the way you wanted me to—even when I don't want to. I'll stay away from people who don't make my life better the way you did. Just give me time. Because I don't know if I'll ever stop loving you. And that hurts almost as much as losing you." My hand slipped away from the frame and my entire body shook with sobs.

Izzy moved to my side and wrapped her arm around me. "Come on. Let me get you out of here." She walked me out of the church and to her car.

I said nothing on the drive to the Fletchers as I stared out the window at the blur of passing scenery. If I didn't think it would hurt their feelings, I wouldn't have even gone. I just wanted to curl up in a ball in my bed and stay there for the foreseeable future.

Once we arrived and stepped inside, it was standing room only. Conversations filled the silence I'd come to know in their home, and people were packed into rooms I'd never even been in before.

"I'm gonna get something to eat," Izzy said as we stood in the corner of the living room. "Do you want me to make you a plate?"

I shook my head.

"You haven't eaten anything other than peanut butter in days."

"I'm not hungry," I said.

I could see the concern in her face, but she didn't push me, heading toward the kitchen.

I glanced around the living room and didn't recognize a single person. I suddenly felt like an outsider in a place I'd come to feel at home in. People smiled and laughed, as if Kyler hadn't been ripped from their lives. Their callous conversations reverberated in my ears until a piercing noise rang out, replacing them.

Sweat beaded on my forehead.

My chest tightened.

I felt as if I was slowly suffocating and needed air.

I rushed toward the basement, bumping into people without apology. I needed to be alone in a place that held memories for Kyler and me. I descended the steps, stopping short on the last step. Bono and a group of guys gathered down there on the sectional. All conversations ceased and all eyes turned to me.

"Great speech, Nora," Bono said when he spotted me.

"Thanks," I said.

"I'm glad you got his heart. It's a strong one."

Tears glazed my eyes. "It is," I said before turning on my heels and heading back upstairs.

I weaved my way through the living room full of strangers until I reached the stairs. I'd never been upstairs, but it seemed like the only quiet place.

Once I reached the second floor, I could breathe a little easier. I moved down the hallway, peeking into bedrooms until I found the one I was looking for—the one with football posters and trophies stacked on shelves. I stepped inside, quietly closing the door behind me.

From the curtains and walls to the comforter and rug, various shades of blue surrounded me. I moved to Kyler's dresser, admiring the football encased in glass in the center of it. I peered through the glass, noticing all the signatures on the ball and the handwritten note—in what I assumed was Kyler's handwriting—stating it was his last high school touchdown ball.

I glanced up into the dresser mirror, shuddering at my gaunt appearance before shifting my focus to the concert and game ticket stubs tucked into the side of it.

I turned away and moved to his bed. I lowered myself down and snatched up one of his pillows, hugging it to my chest. I dropped my nose to it seeking his smell. The familiar scent faintly remained on the pillow case causing tears to prick my eyes. Knowing it was only adding to my grief, I returned it to its place and lay down on his bed. I closed my eyes, trying to ward off the obstinate tears.

The muffled sound of conversations drifted upstairs, and I fought like hell to block it out. Where had these people been while he was still here? How could they smile and carry on while I couldn't get any lower?

"What are you thinking about?" a voice asked.

I froze, my eyes remaining shut for fear of what I might find.

"Because the way I see it, it took me a hell of a long time to find my way back here, and if this is the way you greet me, well that really sucks."

I jolted up with my eyes now open.

Kyler stood there.

I leaped off the bed and stumbled backward until I was on the opposite side of the room from him.

"Hello to you too," he said, looking the same as he normally did except for the faintest glow around him telling me what I already knew. He'd recently crossed over.

"But," I stuttered. "I thought…*how?*"

A slow smile spread across his face as he buried his hands in the pockets of his jeans and took a single step closer to me. "No idea."

"This can't be real." I stepped back, not wanting to get too close to discover he wasn't really there. "*You* can't be real."

He moved closer.

With each of his steps, I grew more anxious. My— *his*—heart beat like a drum in my chest.

He stopped in front of me.

As terrified as I was to learn the truth, I lifted my trembling hand.

"Moment of truth," he said, watching as my hand inched closer to his chest.

I dragged in a deep breath before pressing my palm against his chest. All the air rushed out of me. "Oh my God!" I launched myself into his arms. Luckily, he caught me, wrapping his arms around me and holding me tightly to him.

"How is this even happening?" I cried, savoring the feel of his strong arms around me.

"I hear there's a piece of me inside of you," he said.

I pulled back with tears falling from my eyes. "I'm sorry."

"Don't be sorry. I can't think of a better place for it," he assured me.

"Where've you been?"

"I told you. Trying to find my way back to you," he said with a smile. "And I didn't plan on talking when I found you."

"No?"

He leaned forward and kissed my tear-glazed lips. His tongue pushed its way between my lips for one long, welcome-home kiss. I arched into him, unable to get close enough as the gentle glide of his tongue reminded me of home. I didn't want this moment to end— especially if I was dreaming. But it wasn't me who pulled away first. "Do I need to be careful with you now?" he asked.

I smiled through my tears. "I have the heart of a cocky athlete. I think I'm good."

His lips twitched. "You sure you won't get sick of me?"

"Why would you say that?"

"Because you're stuck with me now," he said.

"So, you won't disappear?"

He shook his head and placed his hand over my heart. "This part of me inside of you assures it."

I worried my bottom lip, still scared to accept this was all real.

"What are you thinking?"

"I'm thinking if this is a dream, I don't want to wake up." Losing him had been torture. I couldn't lose him twice.

"I'm not going anywhere." He lifted his thumbs to my cheeks and wiped away my tears. "But, there are gonna be a lot of things I won't be able to give you."

"I don't care. I've lived without you, and I don't *ever* want to do that again."

He swept me off my feet and held me in his arms. "Say it again."

I couldn't contain my smile. "I've lived without you, and I don't want to do it again."

Dimples dug into his cheeks. "I love you, Nora."

My—*his*—heart was bursting with happiness. "I love *you*."

"I guess nothing in this world could keep us apart, huh?" he said.

"Nothing," I agreed.

EPILOGUE

Two Years Later

The sun reflected off the Caribbean Sea at sunset. It was the perfect backdrop for our special day. I walked barefoot down the sand aisle toward the small altar surrounded by billowing white curtains. I knew I was passing by my mom on my left and Kyler's parents on my right, but I couldn't tear my eyes away from Kyler at the end of the short aisle in a black suit. No more black hoodie. Once you crossed over, you could choose how you appeared to others. His eyes were locked on mine as I moved toward him, my strapless white dress trailing on the sand behind me and my beautiful white bouquet clutched in my hands. My scar from the transplant was slightly visible at the top of my dress, and though most people hated scars, I loved that mine meant I had a piece of Kyler inside of me.

Once I reached him, he held out his hand and took mine. His grip was strong and always comforted me because it was home to me. "You look amazing," he whispered as I stepped beside him.

"You too," I said, before handing off my flowers to Izzy who stood beside Daci.

I turned back to Kyler and we faced the ordained minister—a local medium who could see Kyler.

"It is my great pleasure to be here today to join Nora and Kyler in holy matrimony," the minister began.

"I love you," Kyler mouthed to me.

"I love you," I mouthed back.

I heard his mother sigh. I loved that his parents, my mom, and friends had learned to see spirits—or at least Kyler. It had taken two years, which is why we waited to get married. Kyler had proposed a couple of days after his funeral, but it was important to both of us that our family and friends could be there and actually *see* him. And, they could.

"Love comes in a variety of ways," the minister continued. "Who are any of us to judge when it comes. How it comes. Or who it comes with. If love happens, *that* is the true gift. A gift not everyone gets to experience to its fullest in their lifetime."

Kyler brushed his thumb over the back of my hand.

"Kyler, you prepared your vows. Please take Nora's other hand." Kyler did and we faced each other. "You can share them with Nora now," the minister said.

Kyler smiled, his eyes gazing into mine. "Nora, Nora, Nora."

I laughed.

"You are the most amazing woman I have ever met. You are my safe place. You are my crutch. You are my savior. You came into my life when I needed you the most and blew me away with your strength and determination. I can't imagine spending the rest of my time walking this in-between life with anyone but you. I love you so damn much and nothing is ever going to change that."

Though I smiled, tears glazed my eyes.

"Nora?" the minister said. "Your turn."

I pulled in a breath and exhaled. "Kyler. You are *my* safe place. You are my crutch. You are my savior. You came into my life when I needed you the most and made me see things in a whole different light. You are the love of my life and I can't imagine spending this existence with anyone other than you. I love you like crazy, Kyler Fletcher, and nothing is ever going to change that." A mixture of a laugh and a cry tumbled out of me.

He tightened his grip on my hands, giving me the reassurance he always gave me when I needed it most.

"Do you Kyler take Nora to be your wedded wife?" the minister said. "To love and cherish for all the days of your lives together?"

"Ab-so-lute-ly," Kyler said, and everyone laughed.

I smiled, unable to believe this was my life. It might not have been everyone's definition of normal, but it was the most normal thing I'd ever had.

"Do you Nora take Kyler to be your wedded husband? To love and cherish for all the days of your lives together?"

"Ab-so-lute-ly," I said, and everyone laughed again.

Kyler's smile couldn't have been any wider. Dimples pinched into his cheeks and my stomach dipped at the knowledge that I was his and he was mine forever.

"Who has the rings?" the minister asked.

Izzy handed him two rings.

The minister held them, likely wondering how this was going to work.

"Just put it on the tip of my finger," I whispered to him. "Kyler can take it from there."

He nodded, sliding it onto the tip of my ring finger while I held out my left hand.

"Kyler, repeat after me," the minister began. "With this ring, I thee wed."

"With this ring, I thee wed," Kyler repeated as he slid the ring the rest of the way onto my finger.

I smiled down at the beautiful diamond band that his mother had helped him pick out.

"Nora," the minister began, "repeat after me. With this ring, I thee wed."

Kyler held out his hand and I slipped the ring onto his finger. "With this ring, I thee wed."

I pulled the actual ring back and slipped it onto my own finger as he manifested a duplicate on his finger.

We met each other's gaze and smiled.

"Now, by the powers vested in me," the minister said. "I pronounce you husband and wife. Kyler, you may kiss your bride."

Kyler wrapped his arms around my hips, pulling me flush against him. "Gladly." He leaned down and pressed his lips to mine, giving our guests the kiss they'd been waiting to see.

"Friends and family," the minister announced when Kyler finally released me. "It is my true pleasure to introduce, Mr. and Mrs. Kyler Fletcher!"

Our family and friends hooted and cheered as Kyler took my hand and turned me to face our loved ones. I gasped when I found my father standing in a suit at the other end of the aisle. Tears stung my eyes as I smiled at him. He nodded. I looked to my mother who was staring in his direction, already answering the question if she could see him or not. Izzy tapped my arm, passing me my bouquet. Once I looked back, my father had disappeared. I pushed back my happy tears as Kyler and I made our way down the small aisle as husband and wife.

We spent the rest of the evening dancing on the beach under the stars. Eventually, our family and friends retreated to their rooms, and I was happy to finally be alone with my husband.

Kyler dipped me and I laughed; we were both so happy.

"This day couldn't have been any more perfect," I said.

"I think I might be able to make it even better," Kyler said. "Come on." He took my hand and walked me along the beach. "I want to tell you something."

"Uh oh," I said.

He laughed. "It's nothing bad."

"Okay. I'm listening."

"I got you a gift," he said.

My eyebrows furrowed. "What kind of gift?"

"A wedding gift, though I didn't know at the time that it would be a wedding gift."

"At what time?" I asked warily.

"Um, I think you might need to sit down for this."

"You're starting to freak me out," I said.

"I just need you to hear me out." He tugged me down until I was seated on the sand beside him. "The sacrifices you're making to be with me are not lost on me."

I shook my head. "There's no sacrifice. I want this life. And I want it with you."

He tilted his head, his eyes assessing my face with such love and devotion it still floored me even after two years. "When I was in Florida," he began, "one of my teammates told me about a quick way to make money."

My eyes widened. "Stripping?"

He chuckled. "No, not stripping."

"For what it's worth, I think you'd make a great stripper," I said with twitching lips.

His eyes narrowed. "Okay. But it wasn't stripping. It was making…donations." He winced, awaiting my reaction.

"Donations?" I asked, not understanding.

"To a sperm bank."

My mouth parted as all lucid thoughts came to a screeching halt. "Do you have fifty kids out there?"

He laughed. "No. That's not what I'm trying to tell you."

"Then what?" I asked, wondering where this conversation was going because, from where I was sitting, I had no idea why he felt the need to drop this information on me on our wedding night.

"Every time I…" he winced again, "…made a donation…"

I cringed, the thought of the process downright unsettling.

"The lady at the clinic would ask me if I wanted to freeze any of my sperm. I always said no because why the hell would I need to do that? But, one time, I was like, what the hell. Who knows what the future holds."

My heartbeat accelerated in my chest. "What are you telling me?"

"I'm telling you marrying me didn't make you sacrifice the prospect of children," he explained. "We could have a child together one day."

Goosebumps rushed up my arms as the realization hit me. "You're serious?"

He nodded. "The possibility's there if we want it."

Tears glazed my eyes before trailing down my cheeks.

"Why are you crying?" he asked.

I struggled to find adequate words since I was still trying to wrap my head around the immensity of what he'd unknowingly done. "I knew by marrying you, I'd get *you*. But only you. Which, believe me, I was fine with. But now you're telling me you're giving me something I thought I'd never have. And it would be yours too?"

He nodded.

I cupped his cheeks. "I couldn't love you any more than I do right now."

A smile slipped across his lips. "I'm gonna love you so hard, Nora Fletcher."

"Say that again."

"Nora Fletcher."

I shook my head.

He smirked. "I'm gonna love you so hard."

I moved forward, climbing onto his lap as the waves clapped upon the shore behind us. "Looks like you got all my tomorrows after all."

He kissed me again, and then replied, "And thank god I get all of yours."

The End

ACKNOWLEDGEMENTS

Thank you so much for taking the time to read Kyler and Nora's story. I hope you enjoyed it as much as I enjoyed writing my first paranormal romance!

To all the bloggers, bookstagrammers, booktokers, and readers who share my books. I love you all so much!!

To my wonderful ARC team who read and reviewed *All Your Tomorrows.* Thank you for always supporting me!

To my reader's group, *J. Nathan's Book Boyfriend Lovers.* Thank you so much for loving my books!

To my wonderful beta readers: Amy, Megan, Maria, and Kim. Thank you for always making my work better!

To my editor Stephanie Elliot. Thank you for making my books better! And for being in my head. LOL!

To my wonderful proofreader Peggy. Thank you for going above and beyond to help me put out the best version of this story it could be!

To my wonderful PA Renee. Thank you for always being there for me. You're the best!! Don't let that go to your head!

To Kate at Y'all. That Graphic. You. Nailed. It! Thank you for getting me!

A big thank you to Literally Yours PR for your assistance with this release!

And, last but not least, thank you to my family and friends. I am so lucky to have your love and support!

MORE FROM J. NATHAN

For You Standalone Sports Series:
Book #1 *For Finlay*
Book #2 *For Forester*
Book #3 *For Crosby*
Book #4 *For Emery*

Savage Beasts Standalone Rock Star Series:
Book #1 *Kozart*
Book #2 *Treyton*

Standalones:
Seren
Something About You
I Just Need You
You're the Reason
Until Alex
Before Hadley
Since Drew

ABOUT THE AUTHOR

J. Nathan resides on the east coast with her husband and thirteen-year-old son. She is an avid reader of all things romance. Happy endings are a must. When she's not curled up with a good book, she can be found spending time with family and friends, at baseball games, and working on her next novel.